Carlisle Writers' Group

WRITE ON THE EDGE!

To Brian

Love from

Brenda

Enjoy

Dedicated to
our friends and families

Compiled and edited by
Neil Robinson and John Nevinson

Cover photograph by Nick Robinson

Contents

The result of flash-fiction exercises, some themes – 'The Ultimate Hit' and 'Blue Belladonna', for example - are addressed by more than one author.

Foreword
by Susan Fox

2016 was quite a year for me. Having been a victim of Storm Desmond, I was homeless for nine months, living in five different temporary homes of varying levels of acceptability.

Becoming aware of the stress the flooding causes young children, I wrote *Katie and the Floods* which was distributed to young children in the county (and indeed other parts of the United Kingdom) to read with family and help the talking and healing process. I carried my laptop round to various places and wrote wherever I could find a flat surface and an electric socket. The printing and illustrator costs were met by Cumbria Community Foundation, Rotary and many business sponsors, which was a great luxury. 4,500 books were printed without my having any financial worry!

However, as any serious writer knows, there are lots of other things to worry about; time scales, accuracy of grammar and spellings, clarity and consistency of the plot, suitability of the story for the perceived audience, ensuring illustrations and words fit together with no widows or orphans.

I had thought I was a reasonably accurate, inventive and sophisticated writer until I dared to have my work read by a professional proof-reader friend. On its return there was red pen everywhere. I looked for a 'C minus, could do better' comment. However on reading through the story, I marvelled at the slight alterations, the use of better vocabulary as well as the identification of mistakes that I had not seen when reading and rereading. What a huge help it turned out to be!

It had taken me a long time to have the courage to share my writing with anyone as I was so uncertain and frightened of criticism and rejection. That red pen event changed my mind totally about having the confidence to share work. Why did I not know about Carlisle Writers who could have been my counsellors whilst I learnt to share my stories?

When I was invited to talk to the group, I met friendly and outgoing people drawn together with a common love of writing and interest in each other's work. They were interested in what I had to say and shared ideas and comments with me. It was extremely stimulating and I even went away with renewed determination to revisit a completed story languishing at home.

A bonus for the evening was going away with two books. One was John's short stories. I don't mind that he started the book with a flooding story but the fact that his heroine seems to have had much more fun than I did is difficult to forgive! The second book I took away was Carlisle Writers' previous anthology, *Write Again!* It has so many different writing styles reflecting a variety of interests and is altogether a fascinating read. It really showcases the power of a short story. There is poetry, humour, sadness, a ghost story; a wide range of plots. There is even a evocative flood story, its sharp detail leading me to visualise the scene and smell the flood debris all over again.

All of which makes it possible for me to recommend Carlisle Writers' Group's brand new anthology and to wish its writers every continued success.

Introduction

Carlisle Writers' Group was created nearly thirty years ago by a small band of enthusiasts; its aim was to collect together with like-minded people, giving mutual support and encouragement. Writers come and go, but there is usually a core of two dozen members.

We meet every first and third Monday of the month at the RAOB Club on Fisher Street. One element of the evening is the homework project, where we set, read out and have positive discussions about our work, as well as enjoying writing activities organised by members. CWG is not just confined to these sessions. We give regular readings at the Eden Valley Hospice and local WIs; we have worked in local primary schools; we have been involved in the autumn Borderlines Festival; we have recorded many stories for Radio Cumbria.

And we regularly bring out an anthology of our work. It's three years since we released *Write Again!* in 2014 so there are some new talents appearing for the first time in this new book. Thank you for buying it; your support is much appreciated. You can find out more about us and our work on our regularly updated website at www.carlislewritersblogspot.com

John Nevinson
Chairman,
Carlisle Writers' Group

Susan Cartwright-Smith

Susan returned to Carlisle after an eventful career tailoring in the theatre, and joined Carlisle Writers' Group in 2014. She has previously produced stories to accompany puppet shows in Cumbria, and enjoys writing adult fairy tales, usually with a local slant.

She takes part in extreme folk-dancing, having sustained more injuries in the last few years during clog and longsword dancing, than in the rest of her life.

Susan's children's book *Hairy Monsters & Nerdy Freaks* was published in 2016.

Christmas Story

It was a beautiful scene – the warmth and twinkle of a family's window, dressed in its finery for Christmas. The bright light piercing against the growing gloom of a winter evening. Always a cosy yellow glow. Beckoning. Warm. The smell of cinnamon and woodsmoke overlay the chill tang of the snowy street. Cloves, orange peel, a ham cooking – the olfactory promises of good things. I shivered against the outside cold as the internal fire began to be stoked. This was the kind of scene to make you believe in all the Christmas miracles.

I looked through the window, only half-feeling like it was an intrusion. I could see the comforting scene inside; a Christmas tree, draped any old how, festooned with a mish-mash of lovingly crafted children's decorations, and a more serious attempt at display with fragile baubles and wooden trinkets. The twinkle of lights on the tree, carefully positioned so every bauble gleamed with the reflected beam made my eyes prickle with the winking, twinkling starlit effect. My breath gusted out, like smoke.

I could see a child playing inside; unusual playmates for usual toys as some of the decorations became incorporated into games – camels and kings joining with tin soldiers. The fire glowed in the hearth, the child unaffected by the proximity of the heat.

My hands were cold, holding the packet I had been to collect; streaky bacon from the butcher. Thick rind which would be chopped up for the birds, a rare sight nowadays. A herald of Christmas, preparations for the feast always included wrapping the small sausages in bacon, and other traditions like keeping the goose grease for cooking potatoes in, and locating the silver sixpence. These traditions handed down through time, keeping the past alive. Of such things are memories made.

Once more my breath billowed out like smoke, and I knew that time was slipping away. The image in front of me began to dematerialise like curling drifts of fog, and the reality of the present day setting reasserted itself. The smell of dampened embers became wet leaf mould, the smell of spices just on the edge of senses. A block of impersonal flats took the place of the family home, and what had been my world faded out as a memory. The fire that had raged through from an overlooked candle or a glowing coal had claimed my parents and brother as I collected the butcher's parcel. Nothing left to mark what had stood there but memories and old photographs that no-one looked at any more.

I shiver as a car passes through me. I too am as insubstantial as smoke, curling away like a snuffed out candle. I had run blindly into the street, that night, and had not seen or heard the horses of the speeding fire engine.

Still, Christmas is a time to be with family, is it not? And I have been visiting them for a hundred years now.

Some traditions are to be kept alive.

Sugar And Spice

I wish I wasn't so self-conscious. Can't help it... can't help it. I'm okay. I'm fine. I've been doing well up to now – I think I chose the right frock. Dress. No, I can say frock. That's okay. I think this is... flattering. Not too glitzy. I always feel false. Like I'm trying too hard.

And these shoes – I do feel frumpy in them, but I can't do heels. Not really. Too much. Too tall. And ungainly because I'm not used to them. And I think... I know... that I look odd enough without drawing any more attention to myself.

Who have I been put next to? I always expect to be seated next to the non-challenging blokes. Ugly ones. The ones who either think they wouldn't stand a chance with a *normal* girl, or are unused to any female company, so they don't mind. To start with, anyway. Sometimes they are the most critical. Who is it? Hmm, he's not too bad, actually. I'm not wanting... I don't expect that I will get any, *action,* but, you know, to have a nice face to look at is... Nice.

Sometimes they think I might *want* blokey talk, you know? After the obvious. Like we're so alike, or something. But then, I'm not really an expert at chit-chat. It's like I have to learn it all. A new language, almost. And the little flutters, little flirty things – I can't do it. Well, I've never really tried. Should I try it on this guy? How do I even start without looking like an idiot. Oh wait, he's seen he's sitting next to me. Is he disappointed? There was a bit of a look... just a second, a sort of shrug, on his face. A kind of 'let's give it a go' kind of look. Oh well... let's give it a go, then... sit next to him.

And I think this will be the real test – because now the focus is on *me*. Not my height, or if I've got the right dress on... or if my hair looks too *done*...but now it's *me*! And I can feel them looking. Feel them *staring*, trying to see. Trying to make out the tell-tale signs. And that's why I don't like the whole, what's the word, *flutteriness,* of flirting. I can't bat my eyelashes, I can't put my hand up to my neck. That's the last place I want anyone to look. And I need to be careful with my hands. I'm lucky – I've had a good start, as I'm not too... butch. Used to be teased for being so delicate. But now... Now it's obvious that I'm not delicate. Not in this context. I look clumsy. I look uncomfortable. I feel uncomfortable...in my new skin, I feel uncomfortable.

How I've fought for this. I've fought to be this person. This is who I am now. But I hate feeling people judging me, wondering about me. Those piercing stares, that they think I don't notice. Are they stupid? Heads on the side, staring at my neck, my jaw. Mentally ticking off all the misconceptions they have in their small, small minds. 'Oh, you can always tell,' they say. 'It's the hands, it's the feet, it's the Adam's apple, it's the jawline, the heavy make-up, the stubble...' I've heard it *all* before.

But it's different now. I'm who I should be. I'm reborn, complete. I am me. People can judge me, they probably still do, but it will never be anything I haven't heard before. Sticks and stones? I'm ready. No-one can take this away from me: I am a new…woman. Yes. A woman. I am a woman. I am not that other thing with a handy label or PC term that makes you feel comfortable talking about me. I am right here. In front of you. A woman.

And I'm beautiful. And interesting. And unusual. In more ways than just the physical or the immediate. I have thoughts and feelings and irritations which have nothing to do with operations or tablets or treatments.

And he looks like he wants to talk to me. He hasn't looked at my hands or my neck, or my… lap. He's looked at my eyes.

The Orb

The girl awoke as sleigh bells faded out on the edge of hearing. There was a smell of cold in the air, as if an outdoor coat had been hung in the room. She screwed her eyes shut, but slowly they stretched open again. She lay staring at the line of light which fell across the end of the bed, from the opened door, casting shadows, illuminating an unfamiliar outline hanging from the footboard.

Her toys were as she had carefully arranged them – dolls and bears fleeing from rampant wooden soldiers, while one liveried monkey primly took tea. Various remembrances and reminiscences of her childhood were pinned to the walls. Time pinned in place, described in paints and crayons.

Do not forget.

She pushed the cover down from her chin, slowly, carefully, cautiously. As the cover travelled down her body she willed herself to sit up, eyes drying with the effort it took to keep them open, fear, attempting to shut them. She blinked. On the edge of sight a flicker in the light told her that someone was watching. Waiting.

They could wait.

She crept to the end of the bed. The stocking which hung there glowed from within with an eerie light. She reached out to retrieve it and was surprised at the weight, considering it was so small. Upending it, the item rolled out and spilled its light into the room, blinding her against the darkness. She finally looked up into the shadowed face of the person lurking by the door, and tilted her head in silent enquiry, and beckoned him forward.

"It is what you asked for. The only thing you asked for", she heard him say. His voice was not how she had imagined it would be. Gruff, and cracked, like it had not been used often. Or the tongue was unfamiliar in this head.

"I never expected it to weigh so heavy. I am not sure what I expected. I'm not even sure I had thought I would ever receive it, to know its weight".

"And how does it feel – how do *you* feel, now you have it?"

She crouched down beside it, as it lay on the bed, glistening and glittering, like an oily droplet, light still emanating from it. She studied it silently, hearing the ragged breathing from the cold and shadowed figure, awake to all the sensations of light battling against the dark, cold reaching out into the warmth. She shivered as the frosty tendrils staining the floor reached her, questing outwards from the figure. She inched away, still studying the glowing orb.

"I don't really feel any different. Is that strange? I will keep this though, as I will never get my own back. This will be a useful reminder, and may provide some solace".

She slid it back inside the stocking, and the light receded. She took a moment to glance at the gift tag, and a sad smile twisted her mouth. Her thumb stroked across the gilded lettering; then she squared her shoulders and clenched her jaw.

The visitor by the door faded away, taking the smell of time with them, leaving only the glitter of frost shimmering like tinsel on the tree.

Steve Hubball

Steve moved to Carlisle in 2006 after retiring from his career teaching mathematics in West Cumbria. He joined Carlisle Writers' Group in 2016 with a view to developing his passion for poetry and song-writing, and has enjoyed the very friendly and encouraging atmosphere. In addition to poetry and song-writing, his interests include folk music, singing and playing guitar, art and painting, yoga and mountain biking.

Steve is deeply inspired by mountains and the natural world, and has spent a lifetime climbing the crags and peaks of Lakeland, Scotland, the Alps, Sierra and the Himalayas.

My Table

Here is my table.
A large wooden writing table.
Mahogany? Maple? Rosewood?
I don't know.
I do know it is not a musical instrument.

The table was once a tiny seed.
Imagine. So was my guitar.
Mahogany. Maple. Rosewood.
And the seed became a song.
And the table wishes my song to be sung.

Life Cycles

After the Long Darkness
The Earth Renewer returns
To guide us to the Scorching Summit
Where we can find the Golden Treasure
Before the White Mist settles
Once more.

Rainbows And Floods

Rainbows and floods
The dry earth cries
Who paints the coloured arc
Across the dark sky?

Rainbows and floods
Rivers overflow
Who opened the floodgates
On our small town below?

Rainbows and floods
Icicle cathedrals
Who writes the melody
Of the singing waterfall?

Rainbows and floods
Cars swimming in the road
Who is the weatherman and
What powers do we hold?

Roberta Twentyman

Roberta was born and brought up in the Borders. Now retired, she lives with her husband in Cumbria. Her work is often inspired and influenced by the places where she has lived and worked, both at home and abroad, and the people she has met.

Several of her short stories have been published, as well as the novels *Daisychain* and *In Another Life* and a children's story book, *Tales From Hatcher's Hollow.*

You've Got A Friend

It had been the same as any other Friday night, to begin with. He finished his first set, and acknowledged the applause with the usual finger flurry up and down the keys. It was an appreciative audience. People's requests, and therefore their dollars, had flowed into the huge brandy snifter sitting on top of the grand piano.

He had been about to take his break, when the new arrivals over in the corner booth attracted his attention. He just knew it was her, even though her face was in profile, and the lighting was subdued. As soon as he started to sing, he noted the sharp intake of breath as she turned immediately towards him. A faint smile touched her lips. Her hand automatically started to rise in greeting, then faltered, and instead lingered on the gardenia in her hair.

It had been a long time. Five years. Five years since the lady in the cornflower-blue dress... with the cornflower-blue eyes... the woman of his dreams, first sat by his piano to drink her vodka martini. Here, in the Lemon Lounge.

She had been really sad that night. Makeup hadn't quite hidden the dark shadows under her eyes, nor the bruises on her cheek and arms. He'd asked if he could do anything to help. She'd shaken her head. "All I need is... a friend," was her tearful reply. "Please... just sing..."

He'd bought her a gardenia from the hat-check girl and she'd pinned it in her hair. At last a smile had lit up her face at his choice of song:

Winter, spring, summer or fall,
All you gotta do is call
And I'll be there – yes, I will,
You've got... a friend.

For a couple of hours every third Friday for the next few months, she sat by the piano. Sometimes they talked; sometimes she just wanted to listen while he sang whatever she wanted to hear.

The attraction had been instant, and mutual, but they both knew it could never happen. Never in a million years. She was off limits. This was Baton Rouge. It was the sixties, and *she* was white.

The Wedding Dress

Tracey's Bridal Boutique, although tucked away down a side street in Caldewgate, was without a doubt the best bridal shop in Carlisle, if not the whole of Cumbria. Tracey was not only renowned for the quality of stock she carried but also for the bespoke gowns she created (but only for people she liked). She was just as well known for her acerbic tongue; customers shy of the truth were soon advised to shop elsewhere.

It was into this tiny boutique that the hapless Alison Harrison entered one practically monsoon-like, wet afternoon. She shook her luminous green umbrella out of the shop door before quickly closing it and dumping the brolly on the floor.

Tracey, annoyed at being interrupted, looked up from her sewing machine. "The stand by the door isn't just for show, you know," she snapped. "Kindly get that wet umbrella off my carpet and wipe your feet. In fact – take your shoes off!"

"Oh, s-sorry, s-sorry," stammered Alison, hurriedly slotting the offending article into the stand, while leaving her shoes on the 'welcome' mat.

Tracey stared at her. "Well? What can I do you for?"

Alison smiled nervously... "I, er... I, er... want a dress."

Tracey arched one beautifully shaped eyebrow. "Well, it's lucky you stumbled into a dress shop then, isn't it?" She studied Alison with a critical eye, guessing her to be about 30ish, size 14-16, height 5'2" – and for her age, dumpy and frumpy.

Again Alison stammered and giggled nervously. "Ha... Ha... Yes... isn't it?"

Tracey sighed audibly. "Okay. First, let's establish a few

facts. *This*," she spread her arms wide, "is a bridal boutique. What are you after?" She counted off on her fingers: "A bridal gown? A maid of honour gown? A bridesmaid's gown? I don't do flower girls' dresses – can't stand children, shouldn't be allowed at weddings. Or, are you, God forbid, another nightmare, domineering mother-of-the-bride-from-hell? No, you're too young, I hope!" Alison giggled and shook her head. "Let's start with – is it for you?"

Alison nodded her head vigorously. "I'm the bride," she spluttered. "I'm after a dress – to get married in," she managed to get out, "for me, but I don't want white, or cream – though my mother insists that I do! And I don't want a meringue or a parachute." She drew herself up to her full 5'1" and looked pleadingly at Tracey, "and definitely not a tent." Tracey looked at her with a little more respect.

Alison continued.. "I know I'm a bit overweight, but the wedding's not for another two months. I'll have lost another stone by then." She nodded her head, "Yes. I will. I've already lost one and a half."

Tracey believed her as she had that determined set to her chin and steely look in her eye. Yes, she would definitely do it, and much to her own amazement, Tracey decided she would find the perfect gown to adorn those newly acquired curves. She deserved it. She held out her hand: "I'm *the* Tracey – name above shop. You are?"

Alison grabbed her hand as if her life depended on it. "Alison Harrison." She noted the startled expression on Tracey's face. "I know, I know. My mother thinks she's a poet, and she's rubbish!" Her face flushed with embarrassment.

Rather than cope with the dreaded mother problems,

Tracey quickly took charge of the situation. She put her 'let's get down to business' face on. "Okay, you don't want white or cream. Good! You'd look like a bottle of milk. Come." She led Alison to several racks of dresses that awaited their inspection. Tracey rifled through them apace, discarding one after the other as she inspected the prospective bride from head to foot over the top of her spectacles.

"No, no. Definitely not pink. You'd look like a blancmange. Lemon? No. Give you jaundice. Embroidered? No – a tablecloth. Tartan? No! No! No! Inflated bagpipes. Lilac? No. Geriatric lavender bag. Pale blue? Yuk – a corpse.' She frowned, then out of the corner of her eye she spied the umbrella. 'How about green? A lovely pale, pale green?"

Alison's eyes lit up. "Really? I love green, my favourite colour." Suddenly she looked despondent. "But my mother would have a fit. It's supposed to be unlucky at weddings isn't it? She wouldn't allow it." She hurtled on, as if owing Tracey an explanation. "You see, I didn't have much luck with my last two relationships. First one ran off with my best mate and the second, my cousin Derek! Mother reckons I deserved all I got. Didn't put my foot down enough!" She almost drew blood biting her lip to steady it.

Tracey was gob-smacked. After all that, and putting up with a bitch of a mother, she was still willing to give it another go! This girl deserved a medal; in fact she deserved a bespoke gown. "Alison, you deserve the best. I am going to make you a bespoke gown. You are going to look gorgeous, even amazing, *and* in green. I don't give a flying whatsit for whatever your mother, would or wouldn't allow! You're not ten, and she's not wearing it." She frowned, "What would your intended think?"

Alison took her mobile phone out of her handbag and proudly showed Tracey a photograph. "That's Andy. He's the best thing that's ever happened to me in my whole life." She sighed. "He doesn't really get on with my mother but I absolutely love him to bits." By now, anyone who didn't get on with Alison's mother was a hit with Tracey. "Andy's favourite colour is green too." Suddenly she was overcome with sadness, tears filled her eyes, "but I can't afford one of your bespoke…"

Tracey interrupted. "What's your budget?"

"£750."

Tracey swallowed hard and lied through her teeth. "That's okay. I can work with that," wiping from her mind the fact that a basic bespoke gown was normally at the very least £2000.

The wedding day dawned and Tracey slipped into a pew at the very back of the church. Even she had a lump in her throat as Alison floated down the aisle in a cloud of the palest green chiffon, fitted precisely to every slimmed-down and toned curve. The congregation gasped. The bride was indeed gorgeous, even - Tracey congratulated herself - amazing. She thrust the thought of an anaemic lettuce out of her mind. Well, almost... but at least it was a Kos!

Later, during the photo session, Tracey almost punched Alison's mother who took great delight in muttering in her ear, "Lost three stone and still looks like Shrek!"

"*Shrek?*" Tracey snarled. "That's rich, coming from someone wearing a beige hat, dress, coat, shoes and handbag. In fact, a perfect turd!" However, Tracey did apologise for her clumsiness when she tripped and somehow stabbed a six-inch heel into Alison's mother's foot.

Nothin' Doin'

This short story was inspired by a picture assignment.

The picture was of a painting by Jean Bastien-Lepage (1882) called Pas Meche, *which means 'Nothing Doing.' The painting is of a little boy carrying a long stick and a horn.*

I don't know the location of the painting, but my imagination took me to the deep south. Maybe this is what happened...

Sam, restin' his weary bones on the riverbank, sighed, his reverie disturbed by a bedraggled looking specimen trudgin' his way. He watched the boy from under his hat, through half-closed lids. The smell of the fried chicken wrapped in his bandana stopped the boy in his tracks. On closer acquaintance, he could see the boy was dog-tired, and starvin' hungry. Not a word was spoken.

Sam slowly pulled himself to a sittin' position, offered him the drumstick and a sizeable wedge o' corn bread from his coat pocket - a habit of long standin' when out for a stretch - notin' it took the boy a heap of strength not to snatch an' swallow them whole. Instead, he 'cepted, casual like, noddin' his head in appreciation.

"Where ya' from boy?" queried Sam.

"Up river."

"Uh-huh?" A runaway if ever Ah saw one, Sam thought to himself, and hard though it be, nothin' unusual these days. Times were worse than hard, even young 'uns, through certainly no fault o' their own, were havin' to fight to survive. "Up river, huh?"

"No'th," mumbled the boy, between mouthfuls.

By the ragged state of his clothes Sam was inclined to believe him, "Ah see – bin on the road a while huh?"

The boy nodded, "Yup," he muttered, reluctant to waste time talkin' while he could be a-chewin'.

"Jump a box car?"

The boy nodded again.

Well, that was no'mal. The homeless and hobos spent most their time jumpin' from one box car to 'nother; one railroad company to 'nother. Sam looked the waif up and down. "Them's some boots ya got there, boy. Whar d'ya git them?"

The boy licked his lips, savourin' the last drop of chicken grease and morsel of bread. He dragged his sleeve 'cross his mouth before turnin' his attention to his feet. The boots were at least three sizes too big, but had served him well.

"Got 'em off of a..." he stopped and stared long and hard at Sam before trustin' he could risk further information, "Ah reck'nd he wuz a runaway slave. Name of Efram." Sam raised an eyebrow. "But that ain't no matter." The boy hurried on. "Act'ly, he worried that folks might a thought it odd a slave had shoes. T'ain't civilized." Sam's eyebrows disappeared under his hat. "He was real good to me. Him and Injun Mo. Said Ah needed them more'n him." The boy nodded his head wisely. "Ma momma always reck'nd slaves were white on the inside, same as us. Reck'n she was right!"

Sam stifled a laugh. The boy had obviously had to deal with all kinds of human debris on the road, good and bad. The way things were, he was darn lucky to be alive still. "You tote that pole and horn all the way from up No'th too?"

The boy grimaced but didn't answer.

Sam persisted: "Where'n your folks? On the road?"

The boy shook his head. "My momma died gone last spring." He frowned. "And Ah didn't git 'long with the widda' Clancy."

"The widda' Clancy?"

"I was put in her care when momma died. She took ever 'tunity to whup me with this here hickory stick," - his fingers tightened on the pole - 'fur nuthin'. Said she gonna civilize me!" He grinned. "It's been a fine fishin' pole."

Sam pursed his lips and frowned, imaginin' the pain this skinny runt must've endured. "So – where you headin'?"

"New Orleans – ma Pappy's there. He sent a letter to the widda' Clancy. He's outta jail now, working on the riverboats." His fists tightened, his jaw set. "Sent her money for vittels but 'stead she bought this here horn for her no-good son. He ain't nuthin' but a fool. I reck'n by rights it's mine." His frown disappeared and his eyes lit up, "Pappy'll like it, he can play anything, plays the fiddle real good."

Sam nodded and stroked his chin thoughtfully. "It's a mighty long way to New Orleans."

31

The boy slumped down beside him, unable to stay upright a moment longer. "Ah know, but Ah got it all planned out. Ma Pappy said Ah jes' need foller the river south, an Ah can't miss it."

Sam couldn't argue with that, nor the fact the steel in this young'un's eye would determine he would make it. They stared out across the great river in silence.

"Good fishin, huh?" asked the boy.

"Nah…Nothing doin', not here, but just up river a spell there's a place called Bear Creek, where the fish jump clear out of the water. I guess that's why the bears like it thereabouts. You like to fish, huh?"

"Yup – and Injun Mo. He was from Yucatan. Well, he cooked us a whole mess o' fish over an open fire, best Ah ever tasted." He licked his lips remembering, "What'cha call this here place?"

"This, young sir, is Hannibal. A fine place to hang your hat." The boy listened, a little drowsily, as Sam held forth about the town he loved. "We're sittin' here on the west bank o' the Mississippi near the Fort of Hannibal, in Marion County, in the state of Missouri. Here the river runs deep, that's why they built the wharf just down there. River boats are a-plenty on this stretch o' the river. The paddle steamer with the mail, the ferry over to Illinois, as well as a heap of other riverboats tie up here and unload. Saves a whole heap a time totin' baccy and beef on the Wabash Railroad to and from Quincy, and even St. Louis. It'll make no kind a difference to the sawmills though, their logs'll be floated down river as usual. It sure is big business, the sawmill back there, forest as far as you can see. Black walnut, sycamore, hackberry, cottonwood, wild cherry, pecan, mulberry, oak, hickory, sassafras, linden."

The boy snorted. "Hackberry. Huh!" and spat on the

grass.

"What's the matter? That's a fine strong upright tree. You don't like trees, boy?"

"Don't 'spect you would neither, if ya were borned it." The boy flushed.

"Hackberry? You were a-borned Hackberry?"

The boy clicked his tongue behind his teeth. "Yup, Huckaberry Quinn O'Shaunessy. My momma borned me in a field under a – what she called a huckaberry. Same thing, huh?"

Sam pursed his lips. "Unusual – but could've been worse, could've been sassafras!" he chuckled and clapped him on the shoulder, "Why mine ain't much better!"

"What were you borned?"

"Samuel Langhorne Clemens. Langhorne must a-bin a family name, I guess. For years I thought it was 'Longhorn' – that's a steer." He laughed, shrugged his shoulders and held out his hand. "It's been a real pleasure to make your acquaintance Huckaberry Quinn O'Shaunessy," he smiled. "Hey, be proud, son. Better a strong upright tree than a steer, huh?"

They laughed out loud and shook hands.

Two years later, Samuel L. Clemens, also known as Mark Twain, published a book about a young boy with the unusual name of Huckleberry Finn.

Pat Harkness

Born and bred in Carlisle, Pat is married with three children, two grandchildren and a great granddaughter. She has always had an interest in writing, music and drama, and is a volunteer at the local Green Room theatre. Three of her one-act plays have appeared there, her most recent being an adaptation of Matt Hilton's short stories about the introduction of the State Management Scheme in 1916.

Pat enjoys touring in their caravan, and is a keen baker. "I love a challenge," she says. "My most recent was a sky-dive for charity. Retirement is fabulous!"

Thomas

In the grey half mist that comes just before the dawn, Thomas awoke from a dreamless sleep. Stretching and yawning, he quickly pulled on his trousers, shirt and waistcoat and donned his cap. Shivering in the cold morning air, he made his way down the wooden staircase. The dying embers of last night's fire gave little heat as he ate his bread and sipped his hot sweet tea. He slipped quietly out of the back door to join the others winding their way up the hill.

Standing in line at the coal face, Thomas put on his work clothes before entering the cage that would take him down below the ground at the start of his shift. Stepping out at the bottom, he gave an occasional grunted greeting to his workmates, before placing the heavy girdle around his waist. Crouching on all fours, he began to make his way further down the tunnel, pulling the large container behind him, ready to collect the first load of the day. His feet were bare as it gave him a better grip on the moist, uneven surface. Further and further down he went, the air getting thinner the more he travelled.

The rumbling of his cart joined the cacophony of sounds beneath him, the hammering and clanging of picks against stone. The shouting of orders from the other men joined the whinnying of the ponies and the relentless rumble of the wagons on their never-ending journey. They all toiled in the gloom, man and beast, forcing back the black rubble out of the bowels of the earth. It was Thomas's job to fill his cart and make his way up to the next level. The first load was always the worst, as he heaved and strained to mobilise the cart, cutting his feet on the chippings on the floor, slipping and sliding on the wet ground, until eventually the load shifted forward. He clambered upwards, the soot pricking his eyes and filling his nostrils, hampering his breathing. Slowly, he inched forward; only about forty feet to go before he could unload and make his way back down for a refill.

There were twenty trips to make that morning before he had a welcome break-time to munch on his bread and cheese. Then, it started again - up and down, up and down - no time for slacking. He had to make his quota that day.

"C'mon, Thomas man, put your back in it – c'mon man." Aye, he would 'c'mon'. For the rest of the day he would 'c'mon.' The pace was relentless, but he wasn't cold now. The sweat was glistening on his black face, running down his cheeks making white tramlines against the grime and dust. On and on he went, back and forth, with his heavy burden, muscles aching, heart pounding, legs and arms straining. No room to stand up or turn around, only the constant crouching, pulling, slipping and sliding.

At last it was done. His shift had come to an end. Able to stand at last, he stepped into the cage for the speedy ascent to the surface. No light, though, as he walked outside, for it was night now, and a long trek home awaited him. Still, there was a hot bath and a steaming bowl of broth to look forward to before falling into bed and welcoming blissful sleep.

So Thomas, just seven years old, made his weary way down the hill after another day down the pit.

Keep Me Safe

Keep me safe I beg of thee,
Oh, my beloved hear my plea.
Dost thou not hear my tale of woe,
My beating heart as I watch you go?

With sword held high on your trusty steed,
How canst thou not fulfil my need?
Return, dear Knight, to thy maiden fair,
She with skin of milk and golden hair.

Amidst the maze as darkness falls,
Come lay with me as the owlet calls.
For in your embrace I long to be,
So keep me safe, I beg of thee.

Time's Ticking

The house stood alone on the edge of the cliff overlooking the sea. Tall and proud it had protected its occupants from the elements and the invading sea for many years. It had guarded them through two world wars, but now its last tenant, Martha was preparing to leave. Her family had flown the nest many years before, and her grandchildren were now making their own way in the world.

Martha was old and tired; her bones creaked, her eyesight were poor and she had finally accepted that she could not manage on her own. Her suitcases were packed full of her treasured possessions - photographs, cards, letters, a few paintings. Her jewellery and ornaments were carefully wrapped alongside some toys, baby clothes, shawls and gifts from her family.

It was they who had persuaded her to call it a day. "We worry about you Mum," her daughter Sarah had said. "You're so isolated here and the house is far too big for you." Yes, she knew it, but she didn't want to leave her home, the place she had loved all her life. She sighed as she tugged at her bags, leaving them outside ready for collection.

One last look and then it would be time to go. It had been many years since she had been in the attic, the steep stairs proving difficult to climb, but eventually she made it to the top. The room was large and well lit. Her father had painted his landscapes here, and she remembered her mother puffing up the stairs, just as she had done, playfully scolding her husband for staying there so long. Martha's husband, David, had escaped here when he wanted some peace to read his books, and she herself would sit and daydream busily knitting the children's winter sweaters.

She went down again to the bedrooms, caressing the walls as she went, each room full of its own memories. Dens had been built with an old clothes horse and blanket, hide and seek, and hunt the thimble, the children squealing as they ran from room to room. She smiled, recalling the love and laughter which had resonated within these walls. When she reached her bedroom, the room she was born in, later to become the marital bed, and where she had given birth, the tears began to fall. This would not do, she told herself this was not the time for weeping. She looked out at the stormy sea, land barely visible in the mist.

The sea would eventually claim the house. The cliffs had already eroded the path to her front door. A few hundred yards and the sea would be the victor. It was another reason for leaving

Taking her time she made her way downstairs, passing the old grandfather clock, its tick telling her that there was little time left. In the parlour, the large Christmas tree stood bare except for a tinsel bikini. The wood burning stove flickered as darkness descended. She stroked the walls as she made her way to the last room in the house – the kitchen. Large and colourful, the farmhouse table dominated the room and her favourite place. Such happy times had been spent here, eating, talking, laughing, playing cards and Scrabble and Monopoly. Oh, there had been the squabbles too, the falling out, the making up; it had all happened here.

Martha sat in her mother's rocking chair and poured herself a glass of brandy. The room was warm from the Aga and as she drank, she remembered the past.

She could hear the flames crackling as they leapt down

the stairs towards her, but she was not afraid. The thought of her home standing empty and neglected was more than she could bear. She hoped that her family would understand, that it was right, that they both went together.

She sipped her brandy, smiled and closed her eyes.

Norma Mainwaring

Norma joined Carlisle Writers' Group in the autumn of 2013. She is also the member of a reading group, and records for the Talking Newspaper.

Norma is married with two daughters.

Under The Bed I Found It

There it was again. Maggie sat up in bed with a start: a scratching sound from under the bed and a feeling someone or something was pushing upwards against the mattress. She switched on the bedside lamp and immediately there was silence.

This was the third night it had happened and she had still not mentioned it to Eric who remained sound asleep as usual. Enough was enough; she was going to wake him.

Why hadn't she looked under the bed? Eric had wanted to know. "Well," she admitted. "I'm frightened to." They had rented the cottage a month ago, attracted by the low price and short rental. Eric was struggling with his second book. His agent had told him that this often happened after a first successful novel. Anyway, Eric had thought getting away from it all might help. Ha! Ha! The cottage was cheap and furnished, which was good as they only wanted it for two months.

On examination, the bed seemed fine, an old mattress but clean. That was three days ago. Now this! Maggie shook Eric who awoke reluctantly. She told him what happened.

"Maybe there's mice," he said.

"Well?" she responded.

"Well, what?" Eric replied

"Get up," she hissed, pushing him, grumbling, out of bed. "Help me turn the mattress."

"For God's sake!" He heaved the mattress until it flipped over. It was just as clean on the other side but there were some white marks on the faded blue ticking, which could have been scratch marks. Eric was having none of it. "Hurry up and make the bed before we freeze to death." They lay down again and he was soon snoring. There were no further sounds and Maggie fell into a restless sleep until the sun's rays awoke her.

She pushed her feet into her slippers and, struggling on with her dressing gown, she went downstairs and put the kettle on. She returned with two mugs of coffee and shook Eric awake. "You said you wanted an early start." He was still struggling with the plot. He soon finished his coffee and went for a bath.

"Now," said Maggie to herself, "I'm going to look under the bed and examine the springs." The daylight had made her more confident. The bed was against the wall so she knelt down and inclined her head to look underneath. There was enough height in the old frame for her to get a good view. She was surprised to see a long, shallow metal box against the back wall. She could hear Eric singing loudly in the bathroom so she slid under the bed until her chin touched the box. Maggie had momentarily forgotten her fright on discovering the box so she brought her arms around and gripped the rim of the lid. With a bit of pressure it gradually opened and caught on the bedsprings above. A musty smell of dust, not unpleasant, wafted out, followed by a breath of hot foul air. She gasped as she saw two red eyes peering at her. Then a bony hand grabbed Maggie's neck, suppressing the scream rising in her throat. She felt herself being dragged into the box, the shock making her release her hold on the lid which closed with a click.

In the bathroom the singing suddenly stopped. Eric smacked the surface of the water with delight. "Maggie!" he shouted. "That dream you had last night - I think it might make a plot for my book!"

Maggie heard nothing as she plummeted down and down into the velvet darkness.

Cometh The Moment, Cometh The Man

One by one, the stars began to fade from the sky as a soft glow appeared on the horizon. Slowly and majestically, the sun rose into the dawn sky heralding the start of another day. Gradually, the rays reached out across the land, bathing the city in its already pulsating heat. Moving higher, the sun illuminated a small, square dwelling situated beyond the city walls. The outside steps led up to a door shielded by a thin curtain.

In the room, the rays alighted on the face of a young sleeping boy, as it had done every morning since he was a child. He stirred and stretched beneath the cover. He sniffed the aroma of freshly baked bread and heard his mother singing softly in the room below. He swung his legs out of bed and pulled on a rough tunic. Standing, the boy stretched again, revealing a stocky frame, dark curly hair and nut brown limbs.

He ran down the stairs into the room below, where his mother greeted him with a sweet smile and placed fresh bread and goat's milk on the table before him. He ate hungrily then went about his chores, finishing by cleaning the goat pens and scattering new bedding. His father had left earlier to find pasture for the animals. This had been the boy's job, to tend and keep them safe but a year ago everything had changed. He had been summoned to the palace! A man who worked in the kitchens had heard of the king's mood swings and low spirits and told them that he knew a shepherd boy who played a song like an angel. From that moment, the boy had gone each day to the palace and awaited the king's pleasure. It had been strange at first, as the boy had only ever sung to his goats. However, after a time he and the king became at ease with each other; the lad's playing and singing had seemed to soothe the king, even to the point that the man sometimes fell asleep.

Often the boy spent long periods alone but he was fed in the kitchens and given food to take home which was a great blessing for his mother. His sharp ears soon picked up rumours that the king's enemies were only days away from the city. Then came the day the king sent for him early so he could play soothing music to calm him for the battle ahead.

The boy returned home, strapped on his leather pouch containing a hunk of bread. He did not know that morning, when his mother kissed him on his brow, that this was the day he would meet his destiny.

The Bible does not tell us how David came to be at the battlefield that day but it does tell us that he saw the giant of the Philistines and killed him with his slingshot and a pebble. That day the shepherd boy returned home a man. He did not know then that in years to come he would fight many battles and succeed Saul as king. On his deathbed he would remember only the many songs he'd written and how, a long time ago in a far-off land, a boy named David slew Goliath.

How Are You Feeling Today?

She sits alone as I greet her.
"How are you feeling today?"
Her smile says, "Pleased to see you,"
As she folds her paper away.

Her spirit burns brightly
In a body thin and frail
But her brain is clear as crystal
When she starts to tell a tale.

She is ninety-one and counting,
Her opinions are still strong,
We talk of politics and history,
She never gets it wrong.

She never wanted marriage,
She saved hard to make her way,
"No man will tell me what to do,"
She often used to say.

War came, she joined the WRENS,
Cheered victory hard won.
She travelled the world as much as she could,
And lived life on the run.

She was born into exciting times,
And still has much to say,
So spare some time to listen -
This could be you one day.

In memory of my friend Joyce who died age 92.

Nick Robinson

Nick is originally from the Midlands but moved to Cumbria, which he loves, fourteen years ago. He studied English, sociology and psychology at university and trained to be a teacher.

Nick has been a member of the writing group since 2012 and revels in the ideas which the medium offers. He has always enjoyed imaginative activities.

The Ultimate Hit

Jazz strolled into the gym, swinging the battered door wide, the satisfying slam and squeak of the hinges announcing his arrival. Black, sweat-drenched faces looked up and watched in amazement as the young boy sauntered across the cold, concrete floor. Jazz ignored the grunts of men pumping iron, the Gatling-gun sound that came from the speed ball and the whipping noise generated by the blurred skipping ropes. The whole place burnt with energy as a team of bodies, lifted, puffed, sparred and punched themselves into a whirling hive of action.

The youth passed them all, making a beeline for the far side of the gym, a darker unused quarter. A raised platform loomed up with bright-blue-and-red padded ropes attached to its outer edges. Jazz's slight figure looked so small against the imposing ring, yet he jumped up evading the towering ropes and stepped onto the canvas. He pranced and spun on its surface, like a cock strutting in the hen coop. The youngster's jet-black skin glistened, as he punched thin air. He raised his hands aloft and jumped for joy, letting his imagination get the better of him, dreaming he was champion of the world.

At the corner of the ring stood a weather-beaten, crooked man with a disorganised mess of hair. He leaned on his broom and smiled up at the youngster. "Think you're something, don't ya?" he called out, causing an echo to ripple into the rafters.

Jazz turned around, first stunned then annoyed. "What d'you know, old man?" he retaliated. 'A'int you got no floor to sweep?' Jazz stood up tall, looking down at the the haggard face but the man's grin continued to grow, showing his yellow buck teeth for all the world to see.

"Yup, ya think you're really something. How many fights, you had then, son?"

Jazz put his hands on hips and considered the question, one eyebrow cocked: "I make it thirteen fights so far. I've whupped 'em all."

"Anyone can win against a bunch of chumps, boy. You fought any one good?"

"Denzel Priest!" the boy retorted.

The old man raised his eyes to the heavens. "You mean that tall skinny chump that comes in Tuesdays? The one that can't jab and can't punch? Son, you ain't fought *no-one*! Come down here and I'll tell you something!"

Jazz hesitated for a minute but then manoeuvred himself out of the ring and sat sceptically on its outer apron. The old man tottered forward, swivelled and sank down next to the boy, putting his arms around him as if he was his own child.

"Son, you got yourself a long way to go," he began. "But I like your attitude. You look like you were having yourself some fun in there, fooling around. Let me ask you a question, what do ya think 'the ultimate hit' is in boxing?"

Jazz thought about the question for a while, strangely

seduced by this old-timer's deep, rasping voice. Considering his options, he blurted out "The jab, 'cos it stops chumps from setting their feet. Keeps 'em off balance. Every other punch comes off the jab." Jazz's smile returned as he eye-balled the man.

The older man raised his grisly eye brows, "Son," he said, slowly, "try again."

Jazz, thought hard. "Okay, gramps, maybe its the upper cut, 'cos when it hits the chump on the chin, it's lights out every time."

Rubbing his face, the veteran grimaced as if he'd tasted vinegar. "Son, think harder."

Jazz was now rattled, firing out a response. "Must be the left or right hook to the body then, to get the chump's hands down before I go to the head," but the old man still looked at him like someone with an intense pain in the stomach.

"Son, let me tell you something. It ain't no punch that's the ultimate hit." He hunched over, moved still closer and whispered; a whisper so quiet that Jazz could only just make it out. "The ultimate hit ain't no punch, no siree! It ain't no move or block neither. It don't even happen when the bell goes. The ultimate hit is landed before that hammer goes to that goddamn bell. It's in *here*." The old man jabbed his forehead violently. "Yeah, most fights are won in the head. You see, most chumps can be spooked with some put down, trash talk or jibber jabber. It's down to you to make that chump doubt himself, even before he sets foot in that ring. You gotta put on a show to make that chump feel that you're the hardest 'mother' they've had the misfortune to meet. I'm talking *mean*. It goes two ways though. You gotta make sure you've got the right attitude too. You've gotta think about winning in your head and

49

how ya gonna do it. You gotta see yourself nail that chump a hundred times over in ya head. Over and over. Course, you need some ability and training too, but when it comes down to it, you need to be smart upstairs."

Jazz looked up slowly into the face of the battered, wrinkled man. His impression had changed. For the first time he saw an aged champion. "Yeah," the youth said, standing and turning to go. "Guess I need the smarts."

But instead of moving off, Jazz looked around once more. He hesitated and finally gazed into the old, weathered face. "Maybe you can teach me sometime?" he said.

The Gift

The leather case lay secured on the grass. Its battered tanned cow-hide, brass buckles and poppers glinted in the glow of the waning sun. A boy gazed at the case from a safe distance. He had been there some time wondering why it was there at all. There was no clue of its owner and nothing of interest lay nearby, but here it was! The breeze had begun to get up and the boy shivered, his auburn locks waved wildly as if quaking too. There wasn't much time left in the day, he told himself, and it was now or never.

He neared the locked object, shifting closer and closer. His body slowed and tension rose up as he bent down. His clammy hands stretched out to grasp the strapped case, which swayed precariously in the wind. Straightening his small tense back, the boy took one last look around the wheat-field before picking up the item. It was a good deal heavier than he had estimated but was now in his hands. The boy felt the leather and fingered the buttons. It looked expensive but he could not guess what lay beneath the covering. He drew breath and pulled under the buttons, which made a satisfying clicking noise as he did so, and snapping back the cover. Inside lay two glass discs, sticking out like eyes on a bug, each of equal size, surrounded by rubber trims. Below this, in the darkness of the case, lay dark, metal, angular shafts, while in the middle a singular dial could be made out like that on a radio. The boy was transfixed, scooping the device out with both hands and lifting it into the light. He thought he might recognise what it might be; two small glass circles gave way to thicker pipe-like moulds and ended in larger mirrors of glass. The boy had seen these instruments before in the hands of walkers on holidays. They had been pointing and looking up into far off trees. He remembered now they had been excited and gestured to one another. They had put the instrument to their eyes and stood still, looking out into the distance.

The boy decided to do the same, hauling the bulky device up to eye level and adjusting the optics to suit his small face. At first, he saw only a strange blur of brown and green as he twisted the equipment from one side of the field to the other. Something seemed wrong, he told himself, pulling his eyes away in disgust. After a moment of annoyance, he remembered the dial between the eye pieces and proceeded to tinker with the knob, turning it first one way then the other; at regular intervals he looked through the eye pieces hopefully. At first he had no success, but after he began to lift the device higher and looked further into the distance, he could see images began to emerge from the murkiness. First, a tree presented itself with every knot and bole of the trunk magnified in alarming detail. Pulling away, he gasped at the distance he was from the tree. He tried again panning across to a hedgerow. He could see small white berries on spiny branches and jagged dark leaves embossed with lighter speckles. A bird weaved in and around the hedge, its small wings shimmered and pulsed as if interwoven into the thorny bush. He dropped the device, awestruck by the detailed vision that could be seen from such distance.

The power of the object began to dawn on the child, like the sun rising, submerging worshippers in a radiance of warmth. Kneeling now, the boy feverishly scanned the neighbouring fields and noted the intricacy of ears of wheat and barley. He noticed poppy heads dotted across the edge of the fields and yellow ragwort protruding from the verge.

Then, unexpectedly, he spotted something that came out of the blue. He viewed it in stunned silence. He followed its every step, its every twitch, without the elegant creature even knowing. Its long snout sniffed the air, and then the animal trotted and crouched, its sharp shoulders and thin body emerging from the long grass. Its reddish glossy coat preceded its thick brush of a tail, but it was its eyes that kept the boy transfixed. So near, with the help of the binoculars, but yet so far away! Its deep dark eyes told a story of their own, a story so foreign and alien that the boy would never really know the end of it. The lad flinched for a second, feeling suddenly thrilled and exhausted at the same time, and it was in this instant he lost sight of the fox as it slunk to lower ground.

When the boy returned down the metal road that led to his home, he pondered on the gift that he had found. The marvel of the binoculars showing the world in unimaginably sharp and colourful detail. But then another thought came to him. Were the binoculars the gift? Or was it what lay beyond the lens?

Capercaillie

Death had come to him,
extinguished his last breath,
exiled for books,
and archives.

Black amid the heather,
Out of range, out of sight
Lost in the wilderness,
He survived.

His ancient call and click,
Marked the last lingering place,
Dancing for the dawn
to arise.

Only the frozen countries knew
His deep-throated threat,
Rise and flick of the fan,
His gigantic size.

There has never been another
So fiery and frenzied to fight,
So bold to breed,
before our eyes.

Let us marvel in his second coming,
Rekindled for all of Scotland,
to welcome,
and idolise.

Remembering goes on,
Welcome beaver and reindeer too,
The nation's nature,
Renewing its ties.

Neil Robinson

Neil escaped the University of Cumbria in 2012 and is now working for the best boss he's ever had. This has given him time to publish several books, including two collections of short stories - *Short & Curly* and *Is There Anybody There?* - and others critical of religion. He has won and also been runner-up in two *National Association of Writers' Group*'s competitions.

Neil has been a member of Carlisle Writers for five years. He would like it known, if any famous directors are reading this, that his stories would make really good 'major movies.'

The Night Before Christmas

This story was read on BBC Radio Cumbria in December 2015

Mary sat shivering in the corner. It had been a terrible journey. She was cold and wet and could feel the baby moving inside her. She knew it wouldn't be long before he'd be born and of course she'd always known it was going to be a boy. Joe reappeared with a cup of steaming something and handed it to her.

"Here, drink this," he said, "it'll warm you up." He put his arm round her and pulled her close. She smiled weakly at him and took a sip; some sort of herbal concoction, bitter and sweet at the same time. Joe lifted the shawl back round her shoulders. She wished she was at home and that they hadn't risked the journey, not at this time of year and in her condition. Now here they were on the outskirts of the town from which Joe's family had originally come, and a long way from their village and the little house they'd set up together,

He took the cup from her as she felt the first of her pains and said he'd go and find the landlady to help her with the birth. She'd said she would when they arrived, apologising that, because of the time of year and the big occasion that had brought everyone into town, she couldn't offer them one of her decent rooms; they were all taken, she explained, except the one they now found themselves in. It was cold and had no running water, but was still far better than being outside where the mist was now thicker and icier than it had been only minutes earlier.

"Hello?" Joe called out across the yard, "Can you give us a hand here?" The landlady, who'd introduced herself as Beth King, scurried from the kitchen of the main house, wiping her hands on her apron. The mist parted like the Red Sea as she passed through it.

"Is it time?" she said. "I'll fetch the towels and hot water." Joe had never known why these things were necessary whenever a baby was about to be born but, as they were always called for, he guessed they must be. Beth disappeared again into the swirling fog, emerging moments later with what turned out to be a box of towels and cloths, followed by Mr King with an urn of scalding water.

"Now, don't you men get in the way," Mrs King commanded, taking charge. "Make yourselves useful by..." she paused as she helped Mary make herself more comfortable, "by making yourselves scarce."

"C'mon, son," Mr King said to Joe, "we'll leave them to it. Come and warm yourself up in the kitchen." Joe had thought he wanted to be with Mary as she brought their son into the world, and was shocked, now it came to it, at how easily he allowed himself to be talked out of it.

"You go," Mary said, teeth chattering. "We'll manage." She had reached the point that she didn't care whether he was there or not. She just wanted it over with.

Frank dragged two old chairs across the flagstones and up to the range. He passed Joe another of his herbal infusions. "Not a night for travelling," he said.

"No, indeed," agreed Joe. It was madness really to have attempted it but they'd felt they'd had no choice. They'd felt compelled to make the trip back to the little town from where the Carpenter family hailed. Everything had been fine when they'd left that morning, with a couple of bags each and one for the baby, even though neither of them thought he'd make an appearance quite this early. He wasn't due for another week or two so they were fairly confident they'd be back home before he arrived. It had been a sunny day, if a little chilly, when they'd set off and although Mary found the journey uncomfortable, they were sure they'd arrive before nightfall. But they hadn't counted on the mist that had started to roll in in the late afternoon. Before they knew it, they couldn't see any further than a few feet in front of them, the sides of the road completely obscured. Joe was frightened for his fiancée, her fingers digging deeply into the side of her seat, and for their unborn child. He didn't know what to do; he couldn't stop where they were, wherever that was, but it would be equally dangerous to carry on.

So he was relieved when, through the mist, he could just make out the lights from the farm where even now he sat warming himself. Cautiously, he'd steered them down the track towards the building, somehow avoiding the dark, mist-shrouded ditches on either side and reached the farmhouse without incident or accident. Frank answered his desperate knocking and called his wife once he'd explained that, yes, they did usually have rooms, but that on this night, of all nights, every one was taken. "But you must come in," Beth had said. "We can surely sort something, Frank." And she had fussed about preparing the room in the outhouse, explaining how it wasn't normally used in the winter. But for Joe and Mary it was a godsend, saving them from returning to the road, and a place for Mary finally to rest.

Now, in the drowsy warmth of the kitchen, Frank busied himself stoking the fire and clearing away dishes, while Joe, exhausted after an eventful day, dozed by the fire.

He woke suddenly. A cry from the squat little building outside - a baby's cry. He rushed out into the yard, bumping into Beth in the still swirling mist. "You have a beautiful baby boy!" she cried. "Mother and baby both well. Come and see." Joe pushed passed her and into the tiny space where Mary and his new son waited for him. He kissed her, feeling guilty he had felt so tired himself after the greater ordeal she had gone through. He picked up the little bundle, the baby wrapped in the towels Beth had insisted on earlier. "Take him into the house, keep him warm," she said. "His mum and I will be there soon." If, as he crossed the yard again, Joe had looked up he would have seen the solitary light directly above him, moving slowly across the night sky, the only thing visible through thick, clammy fog. Intent instead on the new-born cradled in his arms, a sense of peace such as he'd never known before overwhelmed him.

He re-entered the kitchen to be met by a veritable host of people: Frank had rounded up his other guests – Mr and Mrs Sheppard and the D'Angelos - to greet the new arrival. "Oh, he's lovely," murmured Agnes Sheppard. "Such a beautiful bambino," cooed Gabrielle D'Angelo, as heavenly voices drifted through the air, the angels themselves marking the birth of this remarkable baby. On the Welsh dresser, next to the radio from where the strains of 'O Come All Ye Faithful' came, the kitchen clock showed it was well after after midnight. Christmas Day; Mary and Joe had a Christmas baby.

Mrs King brought Mary into the kitchen and Joe passed their son to her. Agnes produced a toy lamb from somewhere and perched it next to the baby in the crook of Mary's arm. "It was for my granddaughter," she said, "But I can knit her another one."

"So," said Mrs King, "what are you going to call him?"

"Well, there's only one thing I can call him," Mary said. "He has to be J... J... J," she stammered as nerves and exhaustion finally got the better of her. "We're going to call him J-Justin," she said, "after my favourite singer. Aren't we, Joseph dear?"

Gone Fishin'

We get in the car, me and dad – 'dad and I' as he'd prefer it - and before I can even pull away, he starts.

"So, good night last night?" he asks.

"Yes, thanks," I say. "Very good."

"Anywhere nice?"

"Yes. Very nice, thanks."

"Where was that then?" he asks, angling for more.

"A party at a friend's house, dad."

"A party," he says. "At a friend's house."

"That's right."

"Anybody I know?" he says.

"No, I don't think so."

"Oh," he says. "I used to know all your friends. Once upon a time you'd bring them home so we could meet them."

"They're not a secret, dad. It's just that I have a lot more friends now, a lot of different ones."

"Right."

We stop at a junction and he lets me concentrate on the traffic. It will be a brief respite, I know; the inquisition will start again as soon as we're moving.

Sure enough: "So, is there a... special friend?" he asks.

"Special?" I say.

"Yes," he says. "You know what I mean. A special *lady* friend." He stretches 'lady' to make sure I catch his meaning.

"I have lots of lady friends, dad," I say.

"Oh," he says., "But no *special* lady friend?"

"No," I say. "No-one special."

"Oh," he says again.

"It's okay, dad. I'm perfectly happy with things the way they are."

"Right," he says. Then: "You're not...?

"Not what?" I ask when I realise he's not going to finish the sentence.

"You know what I mean," he says impatiently. "You're not..."

"No," I say. "I don't know what you mean."

He mumbles something under his breath and fidgets in his chair, adjusting the seat-belt.

"It's just... your mum and I have been wondering," he says at last, "wondering when you'll be bringing someone *special* home to meet us."

"Look, dad," I say, "I'm 31, not 16 and I don't live with you and mum any more. I have my own place now, remember?"

"Of course you do," he says, offended, and resorts to silence for the next couple of miles. I'm relieved, but worried I've upset him.

"You okay?" I ask him.

"Course I am," he says. "Why wouldn't I be?"

When finally I pull into the parking area near the river, he's out the car before I switch off the engine. As he pops open the boot he says, "You sure you won't join me? I brought a spare rod just in case."

"No thanks. I've things to do in town but I'll be back for you about five." Besides, I mutter under my breath, I've had quite enough fishing for one day. "Thanks anyway, dad," I say out loud.

"That's okay," he says, clearly disappointed. "You, er... you going to meet... anyone special?"

The Case Of The Vanishing Lady

Neil has written a series of stories about Victorian detective Stanford Wickes, set in Carlisle. This was the first (the inspector hasn't yet been given a name) and is a taster for the forthcoming collection, Inspector Wickes Investigates.

"So whatever happened, it must have happened on the train," sergeant Watkins said.

"It would appear so," said the inspector. "Here's what we know: witnesses saw Miss Dora Gray board the Carlisle train at Edinburgh's Haymarket Railway Station yesterday around noon. The station was, as we might expect, exceedingly busy and several other passengers were able to confirm her presence there. She took her place

61

in the second compartment of the first-class carriage and was, according to the guard, still there at 1 o'clock when he inspected her ticket.

"And yet," added Watkins, "when the train reached Carlisle at a quarter past two, Miss Gray was not on board."

"Indeed," said the inspector. "Once everyone else had left the train, her fiancé, Mr Matthew Tennyson, who had been waiting for her on the platform, reported her absence to the guard. The guard, together with the railway station constable, proceeded to check the train. Both confirmed that the first-class carriage and indeed all of the carriages were quite empty. So the question is, Watkins, what happened to Miss Gray on the midday train from Edinburgh to Carlisle yesterday? I am open to suggestions."

"Miss Gray clearly disembarked at a station somewhere *en route*," Watkins declared triumphantly.

"Alas, no," said the inspector, "the train came directly to Carlisle. There were no stops in between, nor did it slow down or come to a halt for any other reason. Furthermore, if Miss Gray fell from the train, we would by now have discovered her body, so we can rule out that possibility too."

"Well," said Watkins, "evidently between 1 o'clock, when the guard saw her, and a quarter past two when the train reached Carlisle, Miss Gray was killed by person or persons unknown."

"Possibly," murmured the inspector. "And yet that leaves us once again with the problem of a body. There was no sign of one when the train arrived in Carlisle."

"So the murderer took it with him. Didn't the station constable report that a gentleman passenger hailed a porter to assist with a large trunk? The body could easily have been concealed within."

"Indeed it could, Watkins," the inspector said. "But it was not. We were able to inspect the trunk, which the gentleman most conveniently left at the station for later collection. It contained only his belongings from his sojourn in India. There was nothing more incriminating among them than a novel by that reprobate, Wilde."

"So," said Watkins, "Miss Gray did not board the train in the first place. She gave every impression of doing so, but at the very last minute slipped back into the throng at Haymarket."

"You've forgotten the guard who inspected Miss Gray's ticket an hour into the journey."

"Indeed I have, sir," admitted Watkins. "Well, then, there is only one solution; Miss Gray *was* murdered and her body concealed below the seat where it was missed by the guard and the constable."

"It would, I assure you Watkins, have been discovered by now, and it has not."

"Then the murderer, or murderers, returned to the train after the initial examination and removed the body from below the seat to dispose of it elsewhere in the city."

"They would first have had to carry it through the busy Citadel station, past everyone waiting there, including a significant number of railway officials. And, no, before you ask; they could not have removed it via the secret tunnel used by Her Majesty. That, I assure you, was securely locked."

"So, sir," said Watkins quite exasperated. "How was it done? What became of Miss Gray on the noon train from Edinburgh?"

"How was it done?" repeated the inspector. "Quite

easily, I would have thought. At the very time the guard and constable were conducting their search of the train, Miss Gray simply walked through the crowds at Carlisle's Citadel station and out into Court Square. From there she was able to disappear completely."

"She was? How? And how did she avoid being seen by her fiancé... and the guard? Or anyone else for that matter?"

"Oh, but she was seen, by everyone. They did not recognise her on account of her disguise."

"Her disguise? What disguise?"

"As far as I can surmise," said the inspector, "this is what happened. After boarding the train in Edinburgh, Miss Gray waited until the guard had inspected her ticket before drawing down the blind in her compartment and locking the door. She then proceeded to disrobe..."

"Sir!" Watkins objected, "I'm sure she did no such thing!"

"She proceeded to disrobe and to change into the clothes she had brought with her in her suitcase. She also added other elements of her disguise before alighting from the train at Carlisle. After waiting until all the other passengers had disembarked, she then informed the guard of her concern that one had not – meaning, of course, herself."

She informed the guard? I don't understand."

"Yes, *she* informed the guard, who promptly called for the constable to examine the train with him. As they did so, Miss Gray left the station and entered the County and Station Hotel, where she joined her fiancée in a room that had been taken that very morning. It was there, once she had removed her hat and overcoat, that she peeled off the gentleman's wig and whiskers she was wearing and became once again the clean-shaven young man who had boarded the train in Edinburgh."

"Which clean-shaven young man who boarded the train in Edinburgh?" spluttered Watkins.

"The real fiancé of Miss Gray, of course, who, disguised as his betrothed, with a veiled hat to conceal his face and gloves to hide his hands, travelled to Carlisle on the noon train. Afterwards, masquerading as Matthew Tennyson, he reported her disappearance to the guard."

"I see," said Watkins, clearly not. "But why would he do that? Why draw attention to himself and indeed to Miss Gray in such a way? Wouldn't it have been more expedient just to walk away without creating a fuss?"

"But then who would know that Miss Gray had disappeared at all?" said the inspector. "And of course it was important everyone concentrate on the train - that train in particular – and not elsewhere. The young man wished us not to notice that, in fact, *three* people were being made to disappear yesterday."

"Three?" said Watkins.

"Indeed, Watkins; Miss Gray, Matthew Tennyson and the young man himself."

"So Miss Gray did disappear! But if she was not on the train, what became of her?"

"Oh, but she was on the train. Not the one she was seen to be on, obviously, but that which left Edinburgh much earlier in the day. Naturally she travelled incognito, adopting, I am fairly certain, the demeanour of a lady much older than herself. She it was who waited for the young man in the room at the County and Station Hotel."

"How do you know this is what happened?" implored Watkins.

"Because of this," said the inspector pulling from his pocket an object that smelt faintly of spirit gum and looked very much like a gentleman's moustaches.

"This was found this morning in that very room of the hotel. The couple who had occupied it yesterday afternoon left without paying the bill, though the bed, you will be pleased to hear, Watkins, had not been slept in."

Watkins blushed at his superior's brazenness. "But why?" he said. "Why go to all this trouble to make it look as if Miss Gray had disappeared?"

"Aah," said the inspector, "the answer to that is, I think, Gretna Green. Miss Gray's young man, I'm sure we would find, is most vigorously disapproved of by Miss Gray's Presbyterian parents. I'll wager too that if we were to travel to Gretna Green this very morning we might well be in time to apprehend a certain newly married couple."

"Right then, sir," said Watkins, "let us make haste."

"No," said the inspector, "I think not. No crime has been committed, except perhaps for the dishonest use of a hotel bedroom for a few hours. We have, I'm sure you will agree, better things to do today."

"As you say, sir," said Watkins, disappointed there was to be no arrest. "There is, though, something I still don't understand."

"What's that?" said the inspector absently, his attention already on other matters.

"What about her other fiancé - Mr Matthew Tennyson? Oughtn't we, for his sake, to retrieve Miss Gray from Gretna Green?"

"Oh, Watkins," the inspector sighed. "Whatever am I going to do with you?"

Michelle Naish

Michelle has been a member of the writers' group for seven years. She enjoys the friendly encouragement she gets from other members. She loves to write poems and short stories.

Michelle was born in Carlisle where she worked in a nursery for twenty-one years, as well as in factories.

All's Well That Ends Well

Molly looked round her new kitchen. The black marble work tops went well with the red units, and she just loved the new sink. All that was needed now was to have some painting done, but there was no way she could afford to get in a painter or decorator because she had overspent on the kitchen. And there was no way that she could it herself, she just wouldn't know where to start. No, there was only person that she could ask to do the job, and that was her dad.

Molly loved her dad dearly, and knew that she could always rely on him to do little jobs around the house. Well, as long as Molly's mam was there 'to keep a watchful eye on him and make sure that the job gets done right' - these were her mam's words, not Molly's! That's why Molly decided to ask her dad to decorate her kitchen on a weekend when she was working and her mam would be there to keep an eye on the situation. But the very time that Molly fixed for her dad to do the job, her mam was going away on a spa weekend, so her dad would be left decorating by himself.

At first, Molly didn't think much about her mam's

words about her dad, but as the time for the decorating got nearer she wondered why her mam said them. A few days before the job, she asked her mother why she talked about keeping a watchful eye on him. Her mam said that he had once put the wallpaper on upside down, and another time he had put the wrong kind of tiles up; both jobs had to be done again, and ended up costing them more money. "Oh!" said Molly, giving a nervous little giggle.

When her dad called round on the Saturday morning to pick up the colour chart and the keys, Molly made sure she marked off the colour she wanted for her new kitchen. Very reluctantly, she handed over her keys and set off for work. She just hoped that when she returned home, it would be painted the right colour and not sky blue pink, as her gran would say! She made a mental note to phone him in her coffee break, but she just couldn't settle all morning with her mam's words about wallpapering and wrong tiles going round and round in her head.

It was eleven o'clock before Molly got the chance to phone her dad, and it took ages before he answered. "Hi, Dad," she said, sounding jolly but not feeling it. "I forgot to tell you not to let Max into the kitchen while you have the paint out because he always knocks things over off ladders."

"Oh…errr," was the answer her dad gave.

"Oh, you haven't let him in, have you, dad?"

"Of course not!" said her dad. "I know how excited that dog gets. Max is watching me through the back door as we speak. Now I'd best get on, otherwise I won't be finished by the time you come home from work."

"OK, dad. See you later," said Molly, but as she hung up, she had a strange feeling that something was not right. Why had he said "Oh…errrr," and why would he not have

68

finished the small job of painting the walls before she got home? She carried on working through the morning and into the afternoon, wishing her mother was not on the spa break. No, there was no other way. She simply had to ring her dad again, and make up some reason for calling. "But what am I going to say I called for? He'll know that I'm checking up on him." An idea popped into her head and with a shaky hand, Molly dialled her home number. There was no reply. "Maybe he's gone home…" she thought. No. He had said he would see her when she got in from work.

Molly tried three more times to phone him, but there was still no answer. And none from his mobile. All she could think of was that he had fallen off the ladder, broken his leg or knocked himself out. There was that tricky bit of wall just above the door. She could just picture him lying there and Max barking at the back door. Oh, why did she have to work this weekend? Two people were off today so she might finish early. She needed a drink. Just as she was walking into the tearoom, her mobile rang. She took it out of her pocket and was pleased to see her dad's name flash up on the screen.

"Dad! Where have you been? I've been trying to call you for ages!"

"Sorry!" he replied. "I took Max for a walk in the park. Why were you calling anyway? Not checking up on me?"

"No. I just called to see if I can take you to the pub tonight for your tea. My treat for the decorating."

"Yes, that would be nice, love. I'll let you go. I know how busy that shop gets on Saturdays."

"That's OK, Dad," said Molly. " I've got a few minutes of my break left. Just wondering… does the colour I picked look okay?"

"Well, errr…" he began.

"Dad! What's wrong?"

"Nothing, Molly. Best go. Max has just seen a cat. See you when you get in!"

"Dad! *Dad!*" shouted Molly, but it was too late. Her father had rung off. Now, Molly just couldn't wait to get home to survey the damage to her new kitchen.

At six o'clock, Molly entered the house, walked down the hall and slowly opened the kitchen door. She stood in the doorway and let out a scream, not of horror, but of pure joy!

"Dad. It's lovely. What's that colour you've put on the wall? It goes so well with the units!"

"It's called Pearl Grey. I just thought the bright yellow would be a bit overpowering with the red," said her dad.

"You know, I didn't think that, Dad, but you're right. It wouldn't have gone well with the units."

"And what do you think of your floor?" he asked.

Molly looked down at the shiny new grey floor covering.

"Oh, Dad. Everything is so beautiful. Thank you."

"You're welcome, love. And I did all by myself without your mam keeping her watchful eye over me!"

"Yes, dad, you did! And just wait till she gets home tomorrow and sees it," laughed Molly. "I think you'll be busy the next few weeks up at *your* house!"

"I guess so," replied her dad. "Now, did you say something about tea at the pub because I think after all my hard work today, I need a pint!"

"I think so, too," said Molly.

My Dad

A loving warm and caring man,
Who always taught me right from wrong.

Oh, what will I do, now that you have gone?
I promise you I will try to stay strong.

Memories I have, I will hold and cherish,
That is true;
I was so lucky and proud to have a wonderful dad
Like you.

I Don't Know How To Do It!

Tom had loved his time at horticultural college, and hoped to run his own landscape gardening business when he finished. But things didn't turn out that way. He had gone travelling around the world with friends, and then when he returned to his home town of Littlehampton, Tom got a job working in a small garden centre. Soon he met Jill. They got married and started a family.

Tom enjoyed working at the garden centre, and loved giving people advice on what kinds of plants or flowers to put in their gardens. He still dreamed of having his own business, and saved as much money as he could over the years, but with a wife and son to support money was always needed for other things. With a second baby on the way, it looked like his dream was sailing away into the distance. Then suddenly things changed. Tom was made redundant, and although he got some redundancy money, he knew he would have to find another job quickly to support his family. He applied for all kinds of jobs, and attended some interviews, but didn't have any luck.

Tom was starting to feel down about being unemployed. In her usual cheery way, his wife said, "Something will turn up soon, just you wait and see!" Tom just grunted and took Toby out of the back door for his morning walk in the park. On the way home he called in at the newsagents for a paper and, for some unknown reason he did something which he had never done before - he put money on the Lottery. He decided not to say anything to his family. He went shopping with his wife on Saturday, and life went on as normal.

Sunday morning dawned, bright and sunny. "There's a touch of Spring in the air," Tom thought as he set off to collect both sets of parents to go out for a Mother's Day lunch. Later that evening, sitting on the sofa reading the newspaper with his feet up, he suddenly remembered the Lottery ticket in his jacket pocket. While his wife was out of the room, he fetched the ticket and checked it with the television. He had to look at the screen twice to make sure that he wasn't seeing things - but no! It was right, Tom had all six numbers matched. Tom jumped when his wife came back into the room and asked him what was wrong.

"We have just won the Lottery!" he said.

"Don't be daft! We don't do the Lottery!"

Tom handed her the ticket and said, "We don't normally, but I bought this yesterday. Don't ask me why. I just did. Here - check the numbers." Slowly, his wife took the ticket from his outstretched hand, checked the numbers and said, "You're right. All the numbers match. What do we do now?"

Tom took back the ticket and said, "I'll ring Camelot in the morning."

"Oh, Tom!" she laughed. "Just think. Now you can have your own gardening business!"

"I know," he said. "But first things first. Let's get everything sorted with Camelot in the morning. We can take it from there, and see what happens"

A few months later, when everything had been sorted and all the celebrating was over, things started to get back to normal. Tom found somewhere to set up his landscape gardening business, and started to plan how he was going to advertise it. One Wednesday evening, Tom sat down at his computer and started moving the cursor round, muttering to himself. It was a bit loud for his wife who was watching *Coronation Street* and she asked "What's wrong now?"

"I'm trying to copy and paste this stuff but I'm not sure how," he replied.

"Well, just wait till Paul gets in from football, and he'll show you what you need to do. He won't be long."

Tom tried again, and shouted at the computer. His wife said, "I'm trying to watch *Corrie,* and I can't hear a thing with you muttering and carrying on. Go and make yourself a cup of coffee!" Just as he had made them a drink, Paul came in. "Hi, Dad. We won tonight!" Tom waited till his son had told them all about the game before he asked him for advice on how to cut and paste.

"There you are, Dad. It's as easy as that. Have you got the idea now?"

"I think so, son," answered Tom.

"Well, I'm off for a bath and bed. I've got school in the morning."

"Good night, son."

At the living room door, Paul turned and said, "Hey, Dad. I bet when I come in from school tomorrow night you'll say to me, 'Paul. Can you show me how to cut and paste. I don't know how to do it!'"

Tom looked over at his seven-year old son and said, "You could be right!" and thought to himself, "But I do know how to run my own landscape gardening business - at last!"

Marjorie Carr

Marjorie has written poetry from an early age. She is a published poet, many of her poems being inspired by her love of nature. She also writes flash-fiction, short stories and novels. Marjorie has a love of arts and crafts.

She is a life member of Carlisle Writers' Group.

Feeding The Birds

What a delight to see,
Birds visiting the garden and me.
With bread and nuts and seed
They flock around the tree to feed;
And with fat-balls in the holder,
Now the weather's colder.
Sparrow, chaffinch and tit
Cover the branches to sit
And wait their turn to eat.
Their fluttering wings quickly beat,
To balance on the feeders there,
As I watch them – unaware.
Then the woodpecker comes along,
Joining in the fluttering throng.
But the nuts or fat he will seek,
To peck and prod with his long beak.
Much larger – he hogs the holder
Until some birds become bolder,
And try to share the feast.

A Doggy Tale

She was doing that thing with her teeth again. It was so irritating. Like the sound of wellies in crisp snow; compressing and grinding at the same time.

"For goodness sake, eat your toast," I snapped, thinking it would possibly be better than hearing her teeth grating.

"Sorry. I was thinking," she replied, picking up the slice of toast before adding, "The dog barked in the night – and more than once. And if it wasn't barking, it was howling its head off."

"Well I never heard it," I said, but thinking I never hear anything once my head hits the pillow.

"No, you wouldn't. A herd of elephants, trumpeting down the street, wouldn't waken you," she moaned.

I couldn't argue but simply said, "I know."

She munched on her toast for a while, which was preferable to her teeth, before musing, "It must belong to the people at number six. They're the only ones with a kennel in the garden. They likely don't hear it themselves either."

I was growing tired of the conversation and slurped my tea.

"Can't you drink properly?" she complained.

"I like slurping."

She glared at me. "Well, it sounds awful."

I sighed, thinking not as bad as your teeth.

She finished her toast in comparative silence, before addressing the problem of the dog again.

"What do you think we should do about it?"

I tried to plead ignorant. "About what?"

She tutted. "The dog!" she stressed.

"I don't know. Is there anything we can do?"

She wasn't going to let it drop. "Perhaps if you had a word with them," she suggested.

"And say what? Can you shut your dog up?"

"Oh, honestly," she fumed. "Just maybe make them aware of the problem. I can't sleep for it."

She wasn't going to coerce me into knocking on the door of number six. I'd seen the bloke at a distance, all six foot six of him. He was the muscles from Brussels and capable of wiping the floor with me.

"If you can hear it, their neighbours will probably hear it too. They may be on friendly terms with them and drop a hint or two. Just leave it for now."

I could see she didn't like my answer. She had her faults, but I didn't like to see her upset.

"Look, Babs, give it two or three days and then I'll have a word."

I gave her a comforting hug and she cheered up immediately, but I was left racking my brains as to what might happen. Perhaps a pint and a chat with my mates might help.

I needn't have worried. After a couple of days all was quiet, so the neighbours must have said something. Quite possibly the bloke from number five, as I saw him sporting a black eye.

Funny though. A few days after that, we went to the cinema and then on to the Palm Club, for a couple of drinks and the compulsory dance. Who should we find was the doorman but the bloke from number six. Having met him up close really set my teeth on edge, but I was so pleased I had let sleeping dogs lie.

New Fangled

I'm being dragged into the twenty-first century
With gadgets I don't know how to use.
Everything is going digital
Technology we can't refuse.
Computers replaced by laptops,
Or tablets to save us some space,
But cars are now computerised,
With lights all over the place.
Mobile phones have got bigger,
Their screens covered in apps,
Much more than a telephone
Choose anything with swipes and taps.
But you always have to charge them
When the batteries are low,
And it's when you need them most
That the little red light will show.
We now have credit and debit cards
Getting smarter every day.
No need to carry around cash,
Just swipe or tap to pay.
Direct debits and online banking,
Although more open to fraud,
Saves people time and postage.
Writing cheques is mainly ignored.
We program the cooker for meals,
Or the machine to wash our clothes.
Supermarkets now have self-service
But home-delivery grows.
Many buy goods on-line
Instead of going to the shops.
Electric cars and robots.

Innovation never stops.
But if you're getting old, like me,
It is hard to follow the change.
Because of the new terminology,
Instructions are vague and strange.
I've got a laptop and tablet,
An old mobile – way out of date.
I've an HD ready TV,
A digital photo thing I can't operate.
I don't do my banking online.

Lorraine Boyd

Lorraine was born and brought up in Carlisle, as was her father, grandfather and great-grandfather before her (although *his* father came all the way from Brampton). She used to write as a child, when she enjoyed sending her pieces to *Jay's Junior Club*, the children's section of the *Evening News and Star*. Until recently, she worked as an administration officer in the Civil Service.

She is teaching herself to paint using *YouTube*, and became a member of Carlisle & Border Art Society in 2015. Lorraine joined Carlisle Writers in January 2017.

A Faery Story

Long, long ago, in a land where dragons soared over mountain tops, and mermaids frolicked in turquoise seas, there lived a bachelor prince, the only child of an ageing King and Queen.

But the prince was not as princes *should* be, for he was neither gallant nor charming. His eyes were dull, his nose the size of a fist, and his ears stuck out like handles on an ale tankard. And he was petrified of women, not daring to look them in the face. But most worryingly of all, the Prince *detested* bloodshed and refused to attend jousts or battles, executions or stag-hunting, preferring to write poetry in his chambers.

On the Prince's fortieth birthday, the King decreed that the boy have a home of his own. He was given a golden palace, with peacocks strutting among the flowers, and fountains playing on the lawns, and told he must wed.

The King threw a dinner party, inviting all the high-born beauties in the land. "You may pick *any* maiden here as your bride," he commanded, "but you *must* choose *someone* before the clock strikes midnight."

And the ladies piled into the Palace, even those with sweethearts, eager for the chance to be Queen. The Prince stared at his platter, too anxious for hunger. He lifted the knife to cut his sole, but it slipped from his sweaty fingers and clattered to the floor. He could sense the King's eyes boring into him, his mother's disappointed face, the contemptuous eyes of the ladies, and he burned.

Someone passed him a new knife. He looked up to find himself gazing into the bosom of a beautiful serving wench and felt a peculiar tugging in his belly. This, he decided, must be love.

The King turned purple when he heard of his choice, screaming, "Wretch! I will toss you down the oubliette to starve." He stomped about the palace, slamming doors, while his wife and son cowered under the royal bed. For the woman was too menial for a Prince, having been left at the church as a foundling.

But the King was honour-bound to keep his word, and the Prince and maid were married. Wedding bells rang out over the land, and The People feasted on free food, overjoyed with their new Princess Elizabertha. She was of humble origins, like them, so surely she would help The People?

Over the coming months everyone watched the new bride, waiting for her belly to ripen with child. But it remained flat. For a year and a day, it remained flat. For the Princess did not like to share the Prince's bed, and the Prince did not know the secrets of begetting. The People grew restless. They muttered that the girl had bewitched him, that her ignoble blood cursed the union, that she was barren. The old King urged his son to divorce. The Prince trembled, for he was afraid of the King, but terrified of his wife, whose temper grew darker every hour. And so the King told the Princess that her marriage would be annulled, and her title withdrawn. With downcast eyes, she curtsied saying, "As you will, your Majesty."

That evening the Prince took ill. By sunrise, he was dead. Within days, the King and Queen, their hearts in smithereens, joined their son in the family vault.

There were rumours then, rumours that Elizabertha had cursed the Prince, or poisoned him. Riots erupted throughout the Kingdom. The Princess had the Royal Coffers at her disposal and her mercenaries quelled the leaders, beheading them in a grand public spectacle, with free food and wine for The People. The Princess was crowned Queen to loud cheers.

But Elizabertha was never again seen without her bodyguard, Ogred, a giant with the face of a bulldog and fists the size of cabbages, who would tramp behind her, the earth shaking beneath his boots.

The years rushed past, and the Queen's subjects aged and died as all mortals must. And their children and children's children aged and died after them, and so on, even unto seven generations. But the beauty of the Princess did *not* fade and she looked as she had upon her wedding day. The People whispered she was a Vampyre, that she lived by sucking blood, that she had sucked the lifeblood from the Prince.

Then a drought fell over the land, the harvests failed, and The People grew angry. The Royal Coffers were empty, and the Queen could not afford to quell a rebellion. And so, hoping to placate them, she issued a proclamation, saying, "I am in this with you, my people, sharing your suffering. Witches have brought this curse upon us. Let us not suffer them to live!"

So The People dragged the midwives and the wise women and the healers from their hovels and made bonfires of them. But the rain did not come. And The People grew hungrier.

And the Queen said, "Have patience. We are all in this together, I share your suffering. If we all work harder and longer, there will be food for everyone, *next* year."

Then The People shouted, "The Queen feasts and wears fine jewels, while we wear rags and bury our famished children." Revolution was in the air. Elizabertha gathered up her jewels and her gold, tossed them in her carriage, and sped off into the night, Ogred, thrashing the horses until their eyes rolled in terror.

*   *   *   *   *

Some centuries later, a beautiful young widow takes the lease of The Hall, in a village near London. The villagers are suspicious of strangers, and she is a *foreigner* who wears no corset, lets her hair hang loose, and lives without a chaperone. The widow is never in church and is rumoured to have been seen with various men. The gentlemen agree with their wives that, 'the woman's a disgrace'. But when, after dinner, they withdraw to their port and cigars, the talk becomes racier, the bottles emptier, and the widow becomes a favourite topic of ungentlemanly speculation.

Tonight, Lord Humblety is hosting the dinner. "Who'll wager five pounds," he asks his guests, "that I'll bed that widow before Christmas?"

When everyone has left, the drunken lord takes his binoculars and peers across into the widow's window. She has the gas on high and he can see her clearly... my, what a beauty. There is a peculiar twist in his belly. This, he decides, must be love. Perhaps he will contrive an excuse to knock upon her door.

*　　*　　*　　*　　*

A shaft of sunlight bursts through the gap in the curtains and the creature, dazzled by the brightness, blinks at the flowery, feminine wallpaper, wondering how he came to be lying here, on this bed, in this unfamiliar room. This creature has the look of an exhumed corpse, with its withered, grey skin and milky eyes, and it tries to remember how it came to be here. But its brain is slush. Wine. A tight embrace. Then? He is so terribly *weary* and his belly is full of a sick, cold heaviness. He tries to sit up but hasn't the strength, his head flopping back on the fat, feather pillows. Perhaps he has influenza – he is too weak to even reach the bell pull…

Downstairs, the Princess scrutinises herself in her looking glass. Her aura has rejuvenated nicely, turned back from that sickly, cobwebby affair it had become, to this dense, pulsating cloud of vibrant colours. There is still that black patch over her heart, of course; nothing she can do about that.

She had not thought to hunt so near home, but she had been starving for life-energy and he had made it *so* easy. And why worry? There was no mark of injury, no poison in his body; Ogred could carry him back to his own bed and none would be wiser. No blame would attach to her. How could it, when people no longer believed in her kind?

There is no point in feeling guilty. She needs the energy from souls to stay alive. *Everyone* needs a soul. It is not *her* fault she was born without one. Some people just are.

And Elizabertha lives happily for ever and ever after.

The Gift

Lady Harbuckle-Bryce found her husband slumped over his desk. The man was drunk *again*. Afraid of his temper, she shook him tentatively by the shoulder. No response. She touched her fingers gently to his cheek. The skin was icy cold and she knew, instantly, that he was dead.

But she didn't scream or run immediately for help. Instead, a feeling of intense relief flooded her, filling every corner of her body. She buried these wicked sensations deep into her subconscious. Such feelings were most unchristian.

Only after the doctor had pronounced poor James dead, 'of apoplexy,' and the nurse had laid him out on the bed, did Lady Harbuckle-Bryce permit herself to consider her future. Dear James had never countenanced questions as to their finances saying, 'Keep that pointy nose out of my business, Madam.' For as he was fond of reminding her, everything she owned, 'even her own sorry person,' had quite properly come under his sole ownership upon their union.

How much of Daddy's fortune remained? James had been away 'on business,' doing God knows what, for weeks on end, and there had been whispers of gambling and loose women. All lies, of course, she was sure of that. She took a deep breath. Time to find out. She would have to break into his desk.

She felt like a burglar, as she jemmied the locks, and though she knew he was dead, that his body lay empty of any soul in the next room, still her stomach churned with dread that he might burst in at any moment, enraged at her trespass.

The bottom drawer was crammed with papers, and they

spilled out on to the Turkey carpet as she drew it open. They looked like letters. Who would be writing to him? His family had cut off all ties. She picked the first one up and scanned it quickly. It was a love letter. A love letter, replete with salacious descriptions that made her face hot, and romantic effusions of 'undying love.' The letter ended by saying, 'In God's eyes, my darling, *I* am your true wife'.

There were scores of such letters dating back over ten years, along with stacks of receipts for jewellery and clothes that she had never seen or worn. And papers relating to a property in the Lake District, a house she had never set foot in. It seemed that James maintained a second establishment, and a second wife. And all on *her* money!

She could burst with anger. Oh, there was such a rage inside of her, more of it than she could hold behind her tightly-laced up bodice. The energy of it was overwhelming and demanded release. She paced the study, backwards and forwards, backwards and forwards, tearing the letters up into tiny shreds, screaming and crying and thrusting handfuls of the wicked documents into the fire until it choked.

Now she would be expected to enter deep mourning, to arrange an expensive burial with black horses and mutes and a shiny carriage. She would be expected to deport herself with dignity and wear a sad expression.

Well, she wouldn't do it. Just wouldn't do it. She would *not* spend a farthing more of *her* money on that man. She would not waste another day of her life. If his 'true wife' wanted him so badly; she could have him. She rang for the housekeeper.

"Please arrange the purchase of a strong deal box. Lead lined, if you please. I have a rather heavy item that must go by tomorrow's post carriage."

*   *   *   *   *

Annabelle Blythe pecked delicately at her cucumber sandwiches, her Chihuahua, Bo-Bo, begging at her feet. Her corset was pinching most dreadfully. But she daren't loosen her stays. She had to look her best. Any day now, James might come.

There was a tap on the door. It was Mrs Barking, the housekeeper.

"Begging your pardon Ma'am, but there's a man at the door asking if you'll accept delivery of a parcel." Annabelle's spirits soared. Oh, how generous James was! He was forever sending little gifts, *wonderful* gifts.

"It's rather a large one, Ma'am."

The parcel was brought in and laid out on the drawing room floor, and Annabelle went through to inspect it, her little dog clutched in her arms. Mrs Barking was right, the package was *enormous*. What could it be? Bo-Bo wriggled from her arms and dashed towards it, wagging his tail and barking as loud as his tiny body allowed. He began running around and around the box, sniffing at it and whining, as if he was a crazy animal. Anabelle laughed. Bo-Bo was as excited as she was!

The housekeeper came in with a claw hammer she'd found in the cellar, and began to prise open the lid at one of the corners of the box.

Annabelle watched the proceedings, her manicured hands clasped at her chin, her stomach full of pleasantly fluttering butterflies...

The Thing

The digger tore into the wet peat like it was starving. Up in the cab, Sean yawned. The baby had kept them up half the night, so it had. He raised the monster's great neck from its feed, its jaws slavering with peat, and yawned again. It was December, but the sun was warm through the window and he'd had a large pizza for lunch. Best watch he didn't nod off.

But … what the..? His blood froze. A *thing*… six foot… bigger, dangling from the digger's teeth. Trembling, he brushed the peat off the *thing* with cold fingers. It felt peculiar, like chamois leather. His brain struggled to make sense of it.

Then it hit him.

It was a man. A man with a squashed, wizened body. Wisps of peaty hair stuck out from the smashed head, and a single yellow eyeball popped from its socket. Sweat trickled down Sean's spine though he was shivering. "Ah, oh my God… Oh, Jesus! There's been a murder. A body. Jesus."

His supervisor, Bridget, heard his screams and came running up. "What are you screaming about? A body? It doesn't look like a body to me. Just a lump of old peat, so."

Then she saw it; the long arms, the flattened one-eyed head, the broken legs. Her ruddy face paled, her freckles stark against death-white skin. "Jesus. Jesus Christ, Sean you're right. What in God's name happened to him?"

But it hadn't happened in God's name. It had happened in the name of the Goddess, five hundred years before Jesus was born...

*　　*　　*　　*　　*

The Goddess is driving him to heaven in her magic chariot. Outside, snow falls in the darkness, lights glow along the path ahead, guiding them to Otherworld. They speed past bushes, past black skeletons of trees, speeding, speeding on, so fast, so very fast.

An owl screeches. Above them hangs a propitious full moon. He has waited so long for her to come. So many, many, years.

The chariot stops. Instant daylight floods the carriage. A ghostly demon hovers beside him. Its skin as brown and crumpled as an autumn leaf. It stares at him with its one yellow eye and he is afraid.

The dark returns, the demon vanishes, vanquished by the almighty power of the Goddess. The carriage begins to move again...

"Wake up, Erik. Everyone is waiting."

The dream vanishes. Gulla, his elder brother is bending over him, a flaming stick in his hand, the stink of rotten meat on his breath.

"It is morning already?" Excitement stirs in his bowels. It is the day of the Great Ceremony. There will be wild celebrations. Feasting, dancing, drinking. And *he* is the guest of honour.

Erik tosses the wolf pelt aside and stretches his arms with a dramatic groan. It is dark in their wattle home, and cold. His belly gurgles; it is three days since he tasted food. The Priestess had ordered him to fast.

He laces his trousers, belts on his jerkin, and pins up his long, yellow hair. "Do I look well, brother?"

Gulla raises his eyes. "Just hurry up, will you?"

It was a moon past since the Priestess had handed the bowl of bannock breads to the young nobles, and each had chosen a chunk. When Erik had broken his piece, it had had the burnt mark of 'The Chosen One' inside. They'd all crowded around him, then, slapping him on the back and laughing.

The brothers trudge out through the rain towards the magic waters, mud squelching up their ankles. How the wet air chills the bones! The ground is littered with sodden heaps of dead leaves and the sky is the glossy black of wet peat. Rain plashes on the leaves, and the wind howls like a lonely wolf.

Erik worries about the day ahead. All eyes will be on him. They have not told him his duties; they are secret, sacred. But Father has promised that, when the time comes, he will know what to do.

They cross from the mud path on to the springy, softness of the peat moss, the earth dragging on Erik's feet, as if trying to swallow him up, making him puff and sweat, despite the scalding cold. The wind whips him, scraggles his hair, makes his nose run. He can smell wood smoke and roasting boar on the air and his mouth waters.

At last they reach the sacred pool. Oak trees grow around the periphery and balls of magic mistletoe hang in their bare branches. A large fire is blazing. Mist rises from the shallow waters into the grey morning making everything eerie. Goosebumps rise on his neck and arms.

This is the most sacred of places, the doorway to Otherworld, the world where his mother and grandparents live. The place he came from and will return to, one day when he is old or slain in battle.

His friends, his cousins, his uncles, his aunts, the Priestess, his father; everyone he knows is here. There is

Inge, his dearest friend - but he refuses to meet his eye and stares glumly at the ground. What's wrong with *him*? This is a feasting day. A day to make merry. There is no sign of the white sacrificial bull calves.

The pair stop under the largest tree and Gulla rams the torch into the ground. This is the most sacred tree; for its roots begin in Otherworld. His hands are sweat-sticky, despite the cold, and there's a nasty wriggling in his belly, almost like he was afraid! Gazing into the pool he sees a faint, broken image of himself dancing among the ripples, trapped there in the peaty water. The King, his father is whispering with the Priestess. Erik has *always* known her, and she was old when his father was a boy. She has a lipless mouth and hooked nose, and her tiny eyes glitter deep in her skull. She has the look, he thinks, of a prey-bird. Erik stifles the impious thought.

The Priestess holds her hands up to the crowd commanding attention. Everyone moves into a rough circle around her. The King hands her the sacred golden chalice. She raises it into the air, chanting the old words, words long passed from understanding. She lifts it over her head, saluting the rising sun, her long, yellowed fingernails curling around its stem like talons.

Speaking still in the ancient language, the crowd bow their heads in prayer.

The branches creak, as if joining their worship, and through the corner of his eye Erik sees his brother Gulla moving behind him. Why's he prowling about at such a solemn moment?

A thud vibrates through his body.

He gasps, the air rushes from his lungs, and he falls to the earth. Gulla wrenches his arms behind his back and binds his wrists. Erik sucks in his lips, desperate not to display fear, but a strangled squeak of a scream escapes.

"Hush," whispers Gulla, "Hush now, brother, or we will be disgraced."

Fear rises from his stomach, intensifying, becoming unbearable. Warm, green liquid burns his throat, makes his mouth sour. Inside his head, he prays, prays that this will soon be over, prays that he will not shame himself, or bring dishonour. For the songs of the future will retell this story many, many times.

They pull him to his knees and the Priestess forces the chalice between his teeth, its cold rim cutting his mouth as its bitter milkiness gushes down his throat. He splutters, and his head fills with a merciful mist. A noose is dropped over his head, pulled tighter and tighter round his neck, squeezing out the air, it feels like drowning, his neck stings. He hears the Priestess chanting in her singsong voice, how helpless, how alone he feels, he yearns for the mother he has never met.

There is a squall of wind. In the branches above, the last leaf in the old oak twists helplessly, resisting its release, clinging frantically to the branch. Warm urine gushes down his legs, and there is a noise, like pigs at slaughter time. The blurred crowd stand in deadly silence their faces blank, white and staring. He feels a stab of hate and fury. Honour or not, he wants to kill every last one of them.

There is a sickening thump on the back of his head, warm, sticky drops trickle down his neck; he smells the iron of blood, and he falls. They drag him by his arms and legs and throw him, face down, into the sacred pool. Cold water wraps around him like a cloak, biting his skin, creeping into his nostrils and through his open lips. He cannot move, he cannot breathe.

Above them, the wind at last grabs the defiant oakleaf,

and it flies free into the air. And Erik floats from his body and up into the sacred tree, and there he is, looking down on them all from its creaking branches. He feels relief, happiness, peace. His ordeal is over, all of it, that life is over at last. He watches Gulla cutting deep slits into the forearms of the dead body. What on earth, he wonders, is he doing?

And then he sees a speck of light in the distance, and he shoots away from the grove, gathering momentum and hurtling, eagerly towards it. The light of Otherworld. Soon he will be with the Ancestors. It pulls him to it with tremendous force. It wants him, as he wants it, wants it more than any lover. He feels such peace, such love; emotions unknown to him in his short and violent life.

Pictures appear in his mind, like dreams in the darkness: A woman, round-bellied with child, pregnant with him, her face red and wet, straining to release him, for he is stuck inside her body. But he does not want to come out into this strange world of pain and struggle, and he resists. They slit her belly open, pull him out, shout happily that it's a boy.

The moons flash by and he grows to manhood... there he is; learning to ride and fight and kill, his first battle... his walk to the sacred pool this morning...

The pictures fade. And his mother is here, inside the light, glowing, as if of light herself. She holds out her arms to him, smiling, welcoming... he moves towards her...

A backward, dragging, sensation, a sinking fear, and he is plummeting to earth, to the grove... where Gulla is threading hazel withes through those slits in his arms, staking him to the bottom of the pool, trapping his spirit in the Between World. The world that is not of the living, nor of the dead. Sacrificing soul, as well as body, to the Great Goddess, Nerthus.

He slams into his ruined body. Back into pain and suffering. Utterly alone, utterly apart from all creation, from everyone, dead or alive.

"You have made a great sacrifice today, my Lord," the Priestess whispers to the King. "It will never be forgotten."

The King smiles proudly. And the feasting begins.

Not until the next dawn do they return home to sleep off their drunkenness and rest their bursting bellies. No one can remember when they last enjoyed themselves so well.

But Erik can never go home. He must stay here in the bog pool. Trapped by its magical powers, until the Goddess claims him for Her own.

And so, he waits. Moon after moon passes, winter becomes spring, then summer, then autumn, and the harvest fails again. A second hungry winter returns and still he is waiting there. Still She does not come.

Year after year he waits. Every autumn the flowers and leaves die, their withered bodies falling to the pool to rot. Their remains pile up, layer on layer of silt, engulfing the Prince, making him part of the peat bog. He is a shadow, a memory, a kind of ghost. Not dead, not living, inhabiting a dream world where he replays his brief life, unable to leave this mortal world nor join the next.

Two and a half thousand years pass like this. Two and a half thousand years of waiting, waiting for Her to claim him, to free him, to take him to Otherworld.

*　　*　　*　　*　　*

And now she is here.

Bridget reached down and touched the shrivelled body. "Ugh. It feels kind of funny."

"Perhaps we'd better leave it alone." Sean stood up, his

legs wobbly but his heartbeat beginning to steady. He wiped his dirty hands on his jeans. He'd been watching CSI on telly last night. "We could be destroying clues. Contaminating the crime scene, so. It looks like he's been murdered."

"No. No – I've heard about these things on telly. They're called bog bodies. The peat does something funny to them, preserves them, makes them go all leathery. No, this thing was killed *hundreds* of years ago. If we call the police all sorts of folk will get involved. It's archaeology, so it is. They'll want to examine it on site. Cordon it off. Perhaps shut down the moss for weeks. Patrick will go mad and we'll lose pay, maybe our jobs. No. *I'll* take it to the police. What can they say? We weren't to know."

Sean wasn't going to argue. She was his boss. And he'd a new baby to provide for.

Bridget arranged the bog body as carefully as she could on the back seat of her car, its head propped against the window, its one eye looking out, "So it won't be looking at me." It was flat, like a giant toad crushed by a lorry, and its head was broken open on one side, like a split chestnut, but you could still make out the whorls on its elegant fingers. It was hard to believe he'd died all those years ago, that he was once a person, a person with feelings and thoughts just like theirs.

It was growing late and she wanted the bog man delivered so she could get home to the kids, so she could put the dinner on and settle down to *Coronation Street*. They were putting the Christmas tree up tonight. She hoped Conner had remembered to buy the lights. Already the moon was out. A big, full moon. Snow was starting to fall, and she put the headlights on and drove as fast as she dared, the cat's-eyes glowing ahead of them as she turned on to the main road. She shivered, this thing didn't half give her the creeps.

The Goddess is driving him to heaven in her magic chariot. Outside, snow falls in the darkness, lights glow along the path ahead, guiding them to Otherworld. They speed past bushes, past black skeletons of trees, speeding, speeding on, so fast, so very fast.

An owl screeches. Above them hangs a propitious full moon. He has waited so long for her to come. So many, many, years.

Bridget imagined she could feel the presence of the iron-age man filling the car. And the feeling was becoming overwhelming… she stopped the car, put the light on, and checked the body behind her.

The chariot stops. Instant daylight floods the carriage. A ghostly demon hovers beside him. Its skin is as brown and crumpled as an autumn leaf. It stares at him with its one yellow eye and he is afraid.

Of course, she was being silly. Getting as superstitious as her old Mam, she was. The bog man was still there, exactly as she'd placed him. But the light had turned the car windows into mirrors, and his one-eyed face was reflected in the glass beside him, like a ghastly demon. She shuddered and crossed herself. Turning away, she switched off the light, and resumed driving.

The dark returns and the demon vanishes, vanquished by the almighty power of the Goddess.

It was warm and dry in the car, but still, there were goose pimples covering her body, and tingling shivers, like cold snakes, wriggling up and down her spine. She imagined that *the thing* was watching her.

The Goddess has come for me. She has come for me at last.

Len Docherty

Len joined Carlisle Writers' Group two years ago and has enjoyed meeting new friends with contrasting writing styles.

He was in the Civil Service for almost thirty-six years, and was weaned on radio comedy. He has always felt that laughter is the best medicine and tries to include humour in his writing.

Haikus

Rows of empty houses,
Desolation in the air,
Floods leave their message.

Snowy topped Skiddaw
like icing on wedding cake:
Winter Wonderland.

Ration books: gas masks,
Powdered eggs and potted meat,
When I were a lad.

Mandela is dead,
He who crossed the divide,
Black and White are one.

Losing weight today,
Went for a hair and beard trim.
Who needs weight-watchers?

Myriad of leaves,
Variable hues abound,
Picture book autumn.

Write three lines each day,
Just seventeen syllables,
Result: a haiku.

Got writers' block,
Similar to knitting soot,
Chimney needs sweeping.

A plain boring face,
Not introduced to laughter:
Sadness all around.

Torch at the ready,
Dwellings shrouded in darkness,
Electric shutdown.

Honesty is best.
Does my bum look big in this?
Can a dolphin swim?

Daffodil time again.
Yellow heads break the surface.
Wordsworth time arrives.

Death By Haunting

What time is it? I feel like I've been asleep for years and years; maybe I have. Anyway, who's counting? I feel like today will be my day, the best day ever. I feel like I know what's going to happen before the event. I don't think you believe me, but then I am the star of the show. Keep your eyes and ears open. You'll be amazed by the end of this spooky tale.

Tom thinks it's going to be his day today, but he's in for a nasty shock. By the way, I'm Sally, Tom's ex. I always reckoned I was quite attractive for my age. I'm fifty, but I haven't got the body I used to have. Tom's only pleasure these days is his flat green bowling. I have to admit he's a good player, even if he does say so himself. I would describe Tom as short, stocky and nearly bald. Mobile he isn't.

Today is the final of the club championships and Tom is hoping to be crowned champion for the first time, but not if I can help it. His opponent is a relative newcomer to the game, so Tom thinks he just has to turn up to win it. No way, Jose! It's not over till the fat lady sings, and Tom doesn't know any fat ladies. Time to make him a little edgy; a few clouds from nowhere, a noisy wind. That's better. It's amazing the view you get from the ceiling. The lounge could do with a woman's touch - fat chance! Now, then let's get the wind and cloud sorted.

Tom is sitting in the lounge so I push a tray off the hatch into the kitchen. It falls on the floor with a shattering sound, splinters of glass everywhere. Tom leaps to his feet, sweat pouring from his brow. He rushes into the kitchen and returns with a hand brush and shovel. He leans down but overbalances - or so he thinks. Actually, I pushed him.

When he scrambles back up, he has blood everywhere, from the glass. "Why today?" he thinks to himself. Luckily for him, the splinters are in his non-bowling hand. Damn! I didn't make a very good job with that tray!

Never mind, the day is young and I have the feeling that for Tom it's only going to get worse. I take the car keys out of his jacket pocket and put them in the ignition. He'll turn the house upside down, sweat heavily, his hands will start to tremble, and he'll sit down in the chair and tears will follow. He might have left me for that skinny cow, but I was the strong partner in our marriage. I did all his bookwork for the business, and all the family finances. He had a really good building business, until he gave Doris an estimate one dark winter night. I've heard sex called many things, but never an estimate! Wonder if he added extras on when she got her final bill? I never used to be as vindictive as this, but human nature can turn you that way.

He hasn't looked for his car keys yet, and when he can't find them, he'll be a nervous wreck! Ah, there he is, going into the garage, just as I forecast, with his sweaty brow and trembling injured hand. He'll be worse when he finds the keys in the ignition.

"Where did I put my car keys? What else can go wrong today?" Tom looks everywhere he can think of, but the keys are nowhere to be seen. He wonders if he'd left them in the car. "I wouldn't be that stupid. Better make sure."

You wouldn't be that stupid? You left me for that skinny strumpet Doris! Looking at her, Tom should have gone to *Specsavers*: a body like a hat stand, no shape to speak of, tinny voice, short straight hair like a kitchen mop from a distance and close up as well. She always had her nose in the air, but it was to be the death of her in the finish. She had her head so far up in the clouds, she didn't notice the barriers were down at the level crossing. She made such a mess of that lovely locomotive. How good that felt! I always said, "What goes around comes around." He should have stayed with me.

"I can't remember leaving my car keys in the ignition," he says. "What's happening to my life? Tom, this afternoon must be your destiny. You never won the club championship when Sally was forever on your back; this will be for Doris!"

Cheeky sod! We'll see about that. You're at the last chance saloon, matey, and it's closed this afternoon.

"Now have you got everything for the game?" Tom thinks to himself. "Your hands are shaking, man. Keep telling yourself that you will - not might - *will* win. Terry, your opponent, is a new starter, a loser. A bit like Sally. Good job she can't hear what I'm saying!"

Not much I can't. Time for strong winds and a touch of rain methinks.

"Come on," Tom says to himself, "you're going to be late for the game. Check you've got all your bowling equipment: bowls, sweater and shoes. Better get going, as the traffic could be busy, and you're not the world's best driver. Neither was Doris. I never knew she was a train spotter -literally!"

"There's a fair crowd at the bowls, most hoping I'll win," Tom thinks as he arrives for the tournament. "There's no space for a chair. Pleased I don't need to sit down; hovering is my thing. Hither and thither, that's me."

I need a good vantage point, right in Tom's eye line. It'll be worth it just to see the look of terror on his face. *Quelle surprise!* After all, it was at the bowling club that I suffered my fatal seizure. He'll be a while yet. He doesn't know that I released his handbrake slightly, after he got out

103

of the car. It's parked on a slippery slope. I also took his favourite chammy out of his bowls bag. I hope he remembered his heart pills. They'll be needed in abundance today. Wonder if they're on the list of forbidden drugs? Sally, how could you be so cruel?

Oh dear, Tom's car has run into another car in the car park, the president's. They're not exactly bosom buddies; a plus for me and a minus for Tom. He's just realised that his chammy is missing: not happy.

Now where should I hover to get the best effect? Tom has to see me, that's the deal. If I face him, he'll spot me fairly quickly. There's a good crowd here to witness his demise. In a bowling sense, that is.

Good, he's seen me. He's stopped, put down his bowl, and he's wiping the sweat off his fevered brow. He has a look of sheer disbelief on his face. He picks up his bowl again, and takes up his stance. He stands back, rubs his eyes vigorously and takes up his position once more. Time for action. The sky darkens and the wind blows up. Tom's face grows greyer by the second. Sweat pours down his face, soaking his polo-shirt. His body resembles an exploding rain barrel. People all around the green realise Tom isn't well.

Tom looks skyward, as the rain starts to cover his sweat-covered pate, creating an oily covering resembling a plastic rain hat. The bowl drops from Tom's grasp in an eerie slow motion. He's now struggling for his balance, arms outstretched more in desperation than for any useful purpose. Slowly, like a video replay, Tom's bloated body keels over, and makes its journey to his beloved bowling green in the sky. I hear a siren, but from my position, it doesn't look good. Sad to say, he lies there like a small beached whale. Tom is now on the path to the afterlife in the next world, and there's nothing anyone could do to help him. This wasn't part of my plan, Tom, but I can't say I'm sorry. If you hadn't dumped me for Boris - I mean Doris - this would never have happened.

The paramedic is still tending Tom, and I don't know which way I want this to end. If he lives, I get another chance to discredit him. If he dies, it could go either way; he could link up with Doris again or choose me.

The paramedic's putting a sheet over Tom; he hasn't made it. I don't know whether to be happy or sad. Is Doris in heaven or hell, and where will Tom end up? I don't know, but I know a Man who does, so I'd better make haste, and find the answer. When I discover where she is, I can make plans for her. I wonder if a ghost can murder another dead person or not? I'll have to look it up in the bad book. I have to laugh though, I say to myself, seeing as no one can either see or speak to me. I digress, as Ronnie Corbett would say. I did say that Tom didn't have a ghost of a chance of winning the championship. Not a ghost of a chance!

They don't call me Scary Sally for nothing. See you on the other side?

Catflapped

Ooh, that water feels so wonderfully soothing. I could stay in here all night, but how would I get rid of all of those wrinkles? I've tried for years without success. What's that? I'm sure I heard something falling, somewhere in the house. It must be my imagination. I'm on my own; hubby's away and everything's locked and bolted. Suddenly, I don't feel so warm, cosy and secure. The water feels cold, although it isn't. Who can be in the house? I'll have to investigate, but I don't want to.

I'm going to pieces: my teeth are chattering, my knees are knocking. I'm beginning to think Janet Leigh and *Psycho*. I want to scream and shout, but my mouth's dried up. If only hubby were here, he would enjoy the moment. I'm so scared, my goosebumps are having children. Typical! Hubby's away on a self- defence course.

I open the shower-door and creep out, which isn't easy when your feet are stuck to the floor. Please God, don't attack me. I can picture some big rough burglar, throwing me around. I jump in the air. No, I haven't seen the burglar, I just rubbed my bare leg on the hot radiator. I feel faint. My palms are sweaty, my nails are digging in to my bathrobe. Another sound. I jump, and shout out, "Who's there? What do you want?" No reply.

I step out on to the landing and listen, trembling. I can hear nothing. Maybe they've gone. See, I've already increased the number of burglars. We've nothing valuable, except me, and I can't be fenced! Wait! Was that another sound, or my knees knocking and teeth chattering? I enter the bedroom and look out of the window. No-one in sight: no strange cars parked. No use, I'll have to venture downstairs. My hair is stuck to the back of my neck. I'm just too scared to leave.

Suddenly, I hear a crash of either breaking glass or china. Hope it's not my best, I'll kill him. My limbs have frozen again. I feel like an extra in, *The Mummy*. What can I use as a weapon? My black-belt in dust empowerment won't be an asset in this situation. I re-enter the bedroom, and search for a weapon. I pick up a telescopic brolly and a perfume spray. Burglars beware! I go down the stairs one at a time. I try to be quiet, but each stair has its own, individual creak. Nearly down, and no more strange sounds, except for my chattering teeth.

Now, where should I go first? Check the kitchen. No one there. Next, the study. No one there either. Obviously not an academic. I'm putting on lights in every room. I feel like a star; switching on Blackpool Illuminations.

There's only one room left: the front room. I freeze again, and then build up my last ounce of resistance. My sweaty fingers slip round the door and flick on the light switch. The room is bathed in light, and suddenly I see a dark shape flash past me across the room. I find my voice and scream loudly. I collapse on the settee, half dead with fear, half relieved at the outcome.

The dark shape I see miaows in surrender.

"Otis!" I yell. "You'll be the death of me. Why can't you ring the bell like normal folk?" He looks at me, leaps onto the settee and onto my lap where he miaows 'sorry'. Talk about a cat having nine lives. I must have got through nine myself tonight. I'll have to have your cat-flap fitted with a bell. I wasn't expecting a cat burglar! Just imagine telling the neighbours I was cat-flapped.

June Blaylock

Born in South Lakeland, June has spent most of her life in and around Carlisle, and joined the Writer's Group in 2011. She writes purely for pleasure, often placing her fictitious characters in historical situations.

She enjoys sharing her stories with other members of the group, as well as reading at Women's Institutes, the Hospice, and more recently on Radio Cumbria.

June's other interests include gardening and choral singing and she has also been a reader for the Carlisle Talking Newspaper for twelve years.

The Brown Bag

Roger Beaufort could hardly believe his luck as he sat by the window of the Black Bull Tavern. It was a sunny summer's day in 1665 and the innkeeper had just announced the imminent arrival of the stagecoach from London, bound for Sheffield. Minutes later a horn blew and the carriage, drawn by six horses, pulled up outside. The weary occupants stumbled their way into the tap room, while the ostlers unharnessed the sweating horses that trotted eagerly into the stables behind the tavern for a well-earned rest.

As the passengers entered the inn, Roger rose as inconspicuously as he could and left by the back door. He had already shrewdly assessed the situation, gleaning the information he needed; the stagecoach was carrying three rich, elderly couples and a young girl about his own age, together with their luggage which was stowed away on top of the carriage- three wooden trunks and a large brown bag. It was the bag that interested him the most, trunks were rather difficult for a highwayman to carry!

Roger preferred to think of himself as a 'knight of the road!' The Beauforts had come over with William the Conqueror and were staunch Royalists and members of the aristocracy, but he was only ten when Charles I had been executed in 1649. Their Derbyshire home had been confiscated by the Roundheads and the family impoverished. Now Cromwell's rule was over, but at twenty-six, with neither mansion nor trade to rely on, he was living on his wits.

He mounted his horse, Pegasus; their chosen destination was a signpost by the crossroads, five miles away. There was a copse nearby to hide in, a clear view of the countryside, and this was the point where the road branched off to Sheffield; the coach would have to pass this way. All he had to do now, was wait.

Two hours later, he spotted the coach approaching slowly uphill. Roger swivelled his neckerchief over his mouth, pulled on his black mask, cocked his pistols and jumped into the road firing into the air. The horses neighed, rearing up in fright and the coach came to a standstill.

"Get out!" he shouted menacingly to the terrified passengers. "Stand and deliver!" He pushed them onto the grass verge with the point of his pistol. "Now empty your pockets!"

Fearfully they obeyed and the haul produced a beautiful carriage clock, three pocket watches - one on a golden chain- five gold guineas and twenty-one shillings and sixpence. The ladies were also relieved of their ear-rings and necklaces. Not a bad day's work, he thought to himself!

The young lady had not yet responded. "And what about you?" he shouted.

"Please, sir, I have paid three guineas in London for the brown bag and its contents and have only two farthings left. My father is the tailor at Eyam and it contains only a roll of woollen cloth. Please do not take it, it is our livelihood."

"Get the bag down and open it or I'll shoot. I want to see what's inside," he shouted to the coachman.

"You shoot me and it'll be the inside of another bag you'll be seeing; the one they put over your head at Tyburn tree!" retorted the coachman angrily. Roger put his hand into the brown bag and rummaged about, it contained only a roll of cloth as the girl had said. This was no use to him. The passengers got back into the carriage, the girl crying and shaken as the horses turned off onto the Sheffield road.

The next day, Roger decided to go to Eyam and find the tailor's shop. He felt sorry to have frightened the girl and ashamed that he had not behaved like a gentleman. It was only a small village and the premises were not difficult to find; the tailor was sitting cross-legged in the window sewing and the shop was busy. He decided to go another day.

The following day he went again; the blinds were drawn and a huge cross in red had been painted on the door. He knocked and nobody answered.

"What's happened?" he asked a neighbour.

"Tailor's dead," he replied, "died yesterday afternoon. They do say t'plague's been brought from London in a brown bag wi' woollen cloth in it. It's the fleas that spread it; when he shook it out they were jumping about all over t'place! It'll be heaven help us if t'Black Death takes off here!"

Roger's face went ashen white as he remembered delving into the bag. He could hardly expect divine providence to help him with *his* record! He vowed that if he was still alive at the end of the week he would change his ways and steal no more.

After a week Roger was still fit and well and he rode over to Eyam to see the vicar. He confessed his crimes and the vicar said:

"If you truly repent, you are forgiven, and I am bound by my vows not to reveal anything you have told me. However, I now have twenty people to bury - the situation is critical. I will give you another chance and also a job - one that few people would volunteer for! To stop the plague spreading no-one is to leave the village; we have all agreed to remain in isolation whatever the cost! This rule must be strictly enforced. Money will be left in a stone trough, filled with vinegar to sterilise it, at the entrance to the village, in return for food and necessities. Messages can be shouted, but only from a distance of twenty paces. We can have no physical contact with outsiders. You must be there outside the village every day enforcing the curfew if need be, leaving us food and comforts, returning messages and keeping up our morale. This is a big responsibility, Roger, but I think you have the qualities we need. Will you agree to take it on?"

"Yes," Roger replied. The poacher had now turned gamekeeper!

The plague at Eyam continued until the following November, and due to the altruism of the vicar and villagers it remained the only place outside London to be affected. Sadly, 260 of the 350 inhabitants died, including the vicar's wife, but the plague did not spread and the village was finally declared free of infection.

The event had changed Roger's outlook completely. He had learnt the value of life. Now, with the vicar as a referee, there were plenty of honest jobs to be had and empty houses to occupy, both here and in London, but best of all Lydia, the tailor's daughter whose infamous brown bag had first brought them together, had become his sweetheart - and now he could actually hold her hand.

Is There Anybody There?

Oakham Hall is a picturesque Grade 2 listed mansion built in the thirteenth century and just off the M40 in Warwickshire. The house is a magnet for tourists, hosting weddings, pop concerts, children's play park, maze and guided tours; but it wasn't always like this. It owes its popularity mainly to someone who isn't there now and hasn't been for some years.

Peter Quennell, private investigator and psychic medium was having a cup of tea when the phone rang. "Hello, it's Frank Charlton here. We've bought this old mansion, hoping to open it to the general public. Eventually we'd like to feature some unique attractions, which that would appeal to both young and old, but strange things keep happening. We think it may be haunted! We've got a lot of money invested in it. Please can you come and investigate?"

This was the kind of work Peter enjoyed most, already he was feeling excited.

"How about tomorrow morning?" he said.

"That'll be great," said Frank, "we'll see you then."

The following day Peter set out for Warwickshire,

arriving just before midday. His eyes scanned the façade of the building as he approached; you could tell a lot about a place from the outside. Oakham Hall was a big ivy-covered, grey stone building with tall windows made up of tiny panes; at one end there was a crumbling old bell-tower. The river Avon ran nearby and the whole hall was set in five acres of lawns, flower beds and manicured topiary gardens. Frank and his wife Anne were waiting for him.

"What seems to be the problem?" he asked.

"Well, we've only been here three months but twice when I've been walking along the top corridor to our bedroom just before dark, I've felt somebody touch my cheek! Then there are the doors that fly open and slam shut for no reason," said Anne, "but the upstairs drawing room is the worst!"

"What happens there?" said Peter.

"Well," continued Anne, "I laid the fire with paper and sticks, intending to light it after tea, and when I went back it had lit itself and all the logs had burnt away!"

"Are you sure about this?" said Peter. "You didn't forget that you'd already lit it?"

"I'm certain," said Anne, "I was with Frank all afternoon in the gardens. It was such a lovely sunny day. Then, later that evening, we looked at our antique sideboard and found somebody had been scratching the top of it, even though the door was locked!"

"I see," said Peter. "Is there anywhere you can go for a couple of days while I investigate?"

"Yes, Frank's away next week anyway and I'll go to our daughter's," she said. "I'm getting too scared to stay here alone!"

A week later Peter returned and set about investigating.

As far as he could see there were four things to deal with. First, there was the ghostly presence in the upper corridor brushing Anne's cheek; then the scratches on the antique furniture and the spontaneous combustion in the fireplace and fourth, the doors that kept opening and closing. The first three would be easily dealt with; the last was more difficult, he believed.

As he drove up, he noticed that there was a stone coat-of-arms over the doorway and in the middle of it, an ornate rose. Looking through his binoculars he could see that in the centre of the rose was a hole. Further along, among the ivy, his sharp eyes spotted a horizontal slit. This was for ventilation and if the wind was blustery, the pressure could build up through the passages, causing doors to open and slam shut in other parts of the building. He began to feel quite excited. The features in themselves were interesting but if he was not mistaken these characteristics, together with secret code signs he had noticed, indicated the presence of a priest hole. This was used in medieval times when it was a treasonable offence punishable by death to be or hide a Catholic priest. That really would be a significant find. Now where might it be?

He pondered the possibilities as he went back to the drawing room. The room was filled with sunshine and he noticed that a shaft of sunlight, its rays magnified and concentrated like a laser beam by a small uneven fault in the glass of the ancient window pane, was slowly burning a track across the top of the sideboard. This was the culprit and had undoubtedly caused the fire to ignite as well. He remembered how magnifying glasses had been used to light fires in olden days before the use of paper. This one had probably been helped by a sudden sharp draught.

Peter pulled the sideboard out of the way and scrutinised

the fireback, pressing each of the bolts which held the iron plate in place. Eureka! It dropped back to reveal a narrow flight of stairs. Crouching down, he squeezed through into a cramped passageway and descended. It was the first time in almost five hundred years that anyone had trodden here. Reaching the bottom, his torch lit up a doorway; he pushed it open and stood transfixed. It was just as the last occupant had left it.

There was a small bed with a patchwork quilt on which lay a priest's black cassock. Next to it was a simple wooden table and chair with a selection of dried-up pens, paint and brushes. A chink of light from the narrow slit outside lit up the most beautifully illuminated manuscript he had ever seen. At the top left-hand side was a huge capital T inscribed in red and gold lettering, encapsulating the scene of Christ handing St. Peter, the first Pope, the keys to the gates of heaven. Underneath, the words in Latin read:

Tu es Petrus et super hanc petram aedificabo ecclesiam meam et portae inferi non prevalebunt adversus eam. Pater Antonius hic fecit MDL.

(You are Peter and on this rock I will build my church and the gates of hell will not prevail against it. Father Anthony made this in 1550)

He lifted up a small rush mat, underneath which was a loose slab that he eased up. Below it was an escape shaft leading to a secret tunnel, now blocked by rubble. Peter stood speechless and overawed. He wondered what had happened to the courageous priest who had so obviously refused to deny his faith, knowing the fatal consequences. Whatever it was, he had not left in a hurry. The heavy scent of mignonette wafted in through the gap. Yes, there was a presence here but it was not an evil one, rather a feeling of deep peace and continuity. This secret place was probably the most serene priest hole in the whole country.

When the Charltons returned the next day, he was able to show them the secret entrance and explain the build-up of air pressure and how when the wind blew from a certain direction it caused the doors to open. The scratches and fire were caused by the sun and the strange presence on the upper floor was no more than bats in the twilight navigating their way home to the belfry. This could easily be cured by replacing some missing roof tiles.

So there is nobody at Oakham Hall who shouldn't be and so far no one has been able to find out who Father Anthony was. The Charltons have opened the cell and excavated the priest hole's escape tunnel, which is half a mile long and goes underneath the river. It has beautiful echoes and is a favourite place for the many schoolchildren who visit. Sometimes, just sometimes, if they shout, "Is Father Anthony here?" an echoing voice will answer "Here!"

Blue Belladonna

It was the spring of 1861, and the trial of Dr. Montague Pendlebury of Easthampton was nearing its conclusion. It had been long and drawn out, not least because of the difficulty in finding enough suitably impartial men to serve on the jury. Almost everyone in town had come into contact with the doctor at some time, and interest in the case had been so keen that the *Easthampton Gazette* had almost doubled its sales in the last few months.

Dr Pendlebury was tall, spare and charismatic. A man of few words and a lover of the countryside, he boasted the largest collection of butterflies and moths in the area, a subject at which he excelled and had given many popular and interesting lectures; but today was not about fritillaries, it was about suspected murder and speculation in the town was rife. Had he, or had he not, murdered his second wife Henrietta and if so, how and why?

There had been a time when the doctor had been blissfully happy with Sarah his first wife, who was warm hearted, jolly and full of life, but even his skill had not been able to save her from the infection she had contracted after giving birth to their only son Cuthbert. He had been inconsolable after her death. Cuthbert, now nine, attended a boys' boarding school at Newfield Heath, fifteen miles away; every Sunday afternoon his father would drive his pony and trap to Newfield where the matron had prepared tea for them.

He had married again two years ago, this time to an heiress called Henrietta, a small, bad-tempered and sallow-faced woman with straight brown hair pulled back severely in a bun. She wore spectacles with thick pebbled glass lenses and had a liking for gin - a habit he had discovered too late.

On the Sunday evening that she died, a maid had gone into the dining room to collect the dishes and had found her in a state of collapse. The maid said Henrietta's speech was confused and she was rambling on about 'bluebells' before she had lost consciousness and died. The maid testified that Dr Pendlebury was not there at the time, but returned later from visiting his son to find his wife dead and the house in an uproar.

The renowned coroner, Sir Bernard Crabtree, was called

to give evidence. At first, he thought she may have had a stroke, but something was not right. It concerned a half-eaten bilberry tart that was on the table. The cook said Dr Pendlebury had picked the berries himself that morning while on a nature ramble, giving precise instructions that she make a pie for tea. Was Henrietta trying to say 'blueberries' instead of 'bluebells' or worse still 'blue belladonna', another name for deadly nightshade? The berries of this plant were lethal and could be found in the hedgerows at this very time, looking almost identical to bilberries - with the exception that it needed only three or four to kill an adult. Was Henrietta trying to say she had been poisoned? He had also found that there were small amounts of belladonna in her bloodstream.

Next to be called to the witness-box was Jacob, a farm hand. He told how he had been ploughing the ten acre fallow field with a team of two horses in readiness for sowing the autumn wheat. He had stopped at the end of a furrow to adjust the plough and rest his horses when he had observed Dr Pendlebury reaching his arm into the hedge at a place near to where some young pussy willows grew and then putting something into his pocket. Jacob said he was not able to see what it was, but knew that deadly nightshade grew there.

Dr Pendlebury was called for cross-examination. All this time he had sat impassively, occasionally looking at his gold half-hunter and making notes in a scrawling copperplate hand. Yes, he had picked the bilberries and given the instructions to make a pie, hoping to eat the other half for his supper. He had also been in the field by the hedge at the time stated by Jacob. He had noticed a blue Purple Emperor butterfly there feeding on the sap from the pussy willows and had caught it in his hands. Thinking to add it to his collection, he had placed it in his pocket, but later thought better of it and put it back, as he already had one, although not such a fine specimen.

As for the trace of belladonna in his late wife's bloodstream, he pointed out that belladonna was widely used as an opiate by opticians to dilate the pupils before examining the eyes, and that his wife had had this very procedure carried out only the day before. However, he did concede that it would have been very unusual to have got into the system, otherwise he would never have let her go.

The jury found Dr Pendlebury 'not guilty,' as there was not enough evidence to prove beyond reasonable doubt that he had engineered his wife's death. But had he done it? The truth - which he alone knew- was yes! It had been easy to pick a few deadly nightshade berries and slip them into his basket, where they were virtually indistinguishable from the dark, rich, purple bilberries. But why? The reporters of the *Easthampton Gazette* would no doubt draw their own conclusions on all these aspects of the case, but the truth was that Dr Montague Pendlebury had simply got tired of his wife; he could not divorce her and if she died from natural causes he would stand to inherit a tidy sum.

Relaxing at home that evening, the doctor smiled philosophically to himself. Did not every cloud have a silver lining? He opened a bottle of whisky and proposed three toasts; one to blue belladonna, one to the law of double jeopardy, which said a man could not be tried twice for the same crime, and a third to the beautiful lady, matron at his son's school, who was secretly carrying his child!

John Nevinson

John trained to be a teacher in his home city of Liverpool before working in Carlisle primary schools for almost forty years.

While teaching, John had written stories for children, but after joining the Carlisle Writers' Group in 2010, he started writing fiction for adults. He has published two collections of his short stories - *A Sting In The Tale (2014)* and *Nothing Can Possibly Go Wrong (2016)*.

Apart from writing, John likes theatre, cinema, walking, gardening, reading, pub quizzes, local history and genealogy - he has traced his family tree back to Cumbria in 1723.

Out For Lunch

Everything that could go wrong for Stephen happened on that day when he was due to take the mid-morning train from Carlisle to meet up with his old college friend Jack in Newcastle.

Following heavy sleep, Stephen had been shocked out of his doziness when he padded dreamily into a cold perfumed puddle on the bathroom floor; the previous night, he now realised, he had failed to screw the stopper from the bottle of hair shampoo, and the glutinous liquid had run through three drawers of the storage unit, and out across the tiled floor. He threw the sticky soaked boxes of soap, deodorant spray and razors into the bath, and cleared up the majority of the mess with toilet paper before taking a mop to the remainder. The quick irritated morning shave left him with a nick under his chin, and with a piece of bloodied paper handkerchief flapping from the cut, he dressed quickly and then made for the kitchen.

Here Stephen microwaved a bowl of porridge inaccurately, ending up with a stodge which could have filled cracks in a garden wall; he couldn't eat the oaten gloop anyway as the intended green-top milk smelled decidedly off. Opening the wholemeal bread to toast, he was annoyed to find that some kind of giant air-bubble had been baked into the dough, and the loaf was basically fresh air enclosed by a crust.

"What else can go wrong?" Stephen snarled, as he went down the path towards the gate to collect the just-emptied refuse bin from the pavement; three minutes later, he was wiping something disgusting from his slippers, and sniffing across the kitchen floor like a demented retriever as he tried to identify which were blotches of canine muck and what was the brown-marbled pattern of the floor covering.

Setting out into Carlisle, Stephen discovered that he had left his bus pass at home only when the amused driver pointed out that he was proffering his Tullie House Museum card. His annoyance, as he counted out small change to the grinning driver, was curdling below his heart like an expanding ache. It wasn't helped by a girl on a mobile loudly regaling the passengers with graphic details of her hospitalised father's bowel problems, and a teenage boy opposite him picking his nose with dedicated determination. By the time Stephen left the bus at the Crescent, he felt so irritable that he could have started the proverbial fight in an empty room.

At the Citadel station, only one of the three hatches was open at the ticket office, and the six people in the queue in front of Stephen raised their eyebrows at each other in frustration, glancing tensely at watches and the electronic arrivals and departures board. Scurrying along to platform five, Stephen realised that, in his annoyance at queuing, he had forgotten to tell the clerk that he wanted the cheaper Senior Railcard price, and that he had paid a third more than he needed to for his return ticket.

Fuming, as the train trundled out of the station eastwards, he realised that he had chosen the slowest train on the timetable, one calling at every station. At Wetheral, a stocky tattooed man got on with a huge slavering Alsatian, whose stentorian bark boomed intermittently all the way to Haltwhistle; at Hexham, four shrill women boarded, and they shrieked inanities at each other all the way to the Metro Centre, where many of the passengers alighted. Finally, the train crossed high above the Tyne, and arrived at Newcastle Central. Walking through the station ticket barriers, Stephen felt exhausted already, even before meeting Jack outside WH Smiths; he half-wished he had stayed in Cumbria, especially as he knew that Jack was never the cheeriest of company.

Even at college, Jack had been notorious for his hypochondria, and if it wasn't enough to regale friends with his own well-rehearsed aches and pains, the Geordie had a fund of tales about neighbours, cousins and workmates and their various trials and tribulations with varicose veins, bladder problems, congested lungs or (best of all) sudden unexpected deaths in bizarre places like school carol concerts or quiz evenings. "They always thought Ronnie was the picture of health," Jack would nod. "Then he keels over at the gardening club summer outing at Belsay Hall. Heart. Turns out it was just a matter of time." Yes, Stephen was *really* looking forward to the meal and the catch-up with Jack! He felt the glowing core of anger, which had been burning in him ever since he paddled through the shampoo and cremated the porridge, would make him less tolerant of his old friend's medical tales today.

Standing outside the shop, Stephen recalled the hurried scrawl inside last year's Christmas card. *"Thanks for news of the grandchild. Was it girl or boy? Cannot remember!!! Also your cruise postcard. Forget where you got to!!! I couldn't do a cruise nowadays with my labrynthitis/middle ear dizzy problem. In fact, I have had bad year with lumbago, waterworks and Achilles tendon. Wife had had ongoing women's problems and son has had neck trouble from rugby. Auntie Kath in Cullercoats has dementia. Remember Lenny Harrison from Whitehaven? He's dead, and so is Rory Atkinson. Both very quick, but a shock all the same. It's a while since we met, so must fix something. Hope you are keeping well."*

So now they were "fixing something," and Stephen, glancing at the station clock showing just after midday, could think only of the morning's accumulation of irritation gnawing at him and the blessed relief of the 4.23 train escaping back over the Pennines to Carlisle.

"Hello, Steve," said a quavering reedy voice, and Stephen saw Jack standing before him. The voice belonged to a gaunt, whey-faced man whom Stephen barely recognised as his old college friend. Jack proffered his bony hand, which then weakly and clammily pumped Stephen's own up and down.

"Hello, Jack." Stephen attempted a genuine smile. "Good to see you. Now, you're the local so where do you suggest for lunch?"

"There's a nice place up Grey Street, before you get to the Theatre Royal. Bit of a climb, though. Usually has me gasping!" said Jack as the two men walked through the high classical arches of Central Station. "My neighbour Martin just dropped onto the pavement round about here. Pulmonary embolism. Only just turned fifty. Left a wife and a lad just started Uni. Terrible." By the time the duo had reached the restaurant, Stephen had heard about botched root-canal work ("a dislocated jaw, she had!") and a poisoned big toe ("If Micah could have seen a doctor at once instead of waiting three weeks...") The men were offered a table near the long Victorian mahogany bar which had gilt-edged wall-to-ceiling mirrors behind it. They settled themselves down, and Stephen picked up the menu, hoping that by studying it intently, he would encourage Jack to do the same.

"What will you drink, Jack?" he asked. "Or shall we get a bottle of the house wine?"

"Sorry," Jack grimaced, "but it'll have to be fruit juice, Steve. I was getting continual bad pains in the kidney area and the practice nurse suggested a few weeks off the vino. Two years now, and haven't regretted it."

"Okay," said Stephen. "Well, as this is my treat..."

"Oh, no, man!" began Jack.

"My treat," Stephen cut in. "You know this place, so what do you recommend?" It was a question which he regretted. Jack proceeded to hold forth, and in his admonitory lecture he mixed facts about unsuitable foods with examples of their dire consequences - his secretary's niece who had a fishbone wedged in her throat, the Welsh guy from the golf club who was violently ill after mussels, the hen party from Blaydon that all went down with listeria... Stephen felt the knot of vexation and anger twist and turn within him as he watched Jack attach a warning story to each item on the menu. "Sea bass. That's what they *say.* But there's that substitute they mentioned in *The Mail On Sunday,* from fish farms in Cambodia or Viet Nam. Well, I ask you…"

"I asked *you,"* said Stephen, more forcefully than he intended. "What do you want for your bloody lunch?" Jack looked rather shocked by his vehemence, so Stephen tried to defuse any tension by saying, "Sorry. I had a lousy breakfast before leaving early for the train, Jack, so I am starving. So, come on, mate, what are you having?" Fearing another lecture, Stephen added, "What do you *usually* have here?" Jack ran a finger down the menu, and went for some vegetarian concoction full of pulses and lentils that Stephen had never heard of, and certainly would never want to eat. Stephen made to move to the bar, but a smart-looking girl came up and said, "Hi, guys, I'm Imogen. Are you ready to order?"

The order placed, the conversation became a little desultory, as they meandered through Brexit, Rafa's tenure at St James's Park, the benefits of Netflix… Then Stephen said, "Did any of our crowd stay on to work on Tyneside? I mean, you were a local anyway, but the others?" It was a fatal question. "Brian stayed on, but he had a stroke and finished work," replied Jack, and then he warmed to his theme. "Maggie Hooper got a house in Tynemouth but she liked the pop too much, and Debenhams fired her. *Serious* problem there. And Adam, that London lad who lodged with Mrs Robson in Heaton, his eyesight was never the same after a smash on the A1 outside Alnwick. And I heard that…"

Imogen mercifully arrived with the two meals - Stephen's overloaded plate smoking and spluttering with a huge gammon steak, pineapple, fried eggs, chips, tomatoes, peas, mushrooms and onions, and the ascetic platter of Jack's pulses, lettuce, peppers, couscous, mackerel and cucumber. Jack stared at Stephen's plate with barely concealed distaste, and suddenly Stephen felt the day's anger come boiling to the surface. He was just about to unburden his ire and snarl, "You prissy little health freak - stop judging my food, my lifestyle… in fact, me" when Jack stared at him, dropped his fork, gasped and began to slide from the chair under the table; the plate clattered down with him, and he fell to the floor covered in food.

Stephen leapt up to call for help, but Imogen and a burly barman were already at the table, and kneeling by ashen-faced Jack. "He's trying to talk," said the waitress, who then tried to hush Jack who was becoming quite distressed.

"Don't speak, Jack," said Stephen, kneeling by his friend. He felt his head pound and something under his ribs thumped alarmingly.

"This… all this isn't fair," Jack whispered. "I eat healthy stuff. Really, *you're* the one who should be ill."

Stephen could see abstemious Jack's point.

"When you tell our friends," gurgled Jack with a sigh, "say what happened. Tell them I was eating properly and you… you… you…."

Jack's head slumped. Stephen remembered all this when contacting mutual friends on Facebook that weekend. "*Sad news to pass on. Jack Rutherford died unexpectedly last Wednesday. Apparently, he'd been severely weakened by following a fairly odd faddish diet for several years. It's a warning to us all. A wake-up call. Live for the moment, folks!*"

You Have Got To Hear This One

This true story was read on BBC Radio Cumbria
in December 2016

Christmas was going to be very different this year. For the first time in our lives, we were not all going to be together for the holiday - my sister's husband had just had a cataract operation and wasn't able to drive north to Carlisle, and Mum was becoming too frail to sally forth on the packed trains to Manchester. It would seem a sadly depleted table on Christmas Day so, as we were breaking with tradition, I decided Mum and I would have our first-ever Christmas dinner out. A table for two was reserved at a swish hotel in the Eden Valley and, as I'm not a driver, a taxi was booked to ferry us out and home again on Christmas Day.

I went over to my mother's bungalow after breakfast, and we had a leisurely Christmas morning. At midday, our usual friendly taxi driver arrived as prompt as he always was. Danny was the ideal man for the day; he was barrel-chested, florid-faced, white-bearded, twinkle-eyed and mischievously funny. He dropped us at the hotel door and said he would be back about 2.30.

Mum and I were greeted in the entrance hall, and I placed our coats up on the tree-like coat rack, one of those upright wooden ones with several arms branching out. Already three or four coats were hanging there. I escorted Mum to the bar area for a drink, and within minutes we were taken to our table in the seasonally-decorated conservatory. Soon we were tucking in to a delicious Christmas dinner, served by friendly staff, and the fact that everything was so different from our usual family day was made easier by the novelty of the surroundings.

Just after two o'clock, full of turkey and Christmas pudding (and a little wine!) we went into the lounge, and eased ourselves dozily into the comfy chairs. It seemed we hadn't been there for five minutes when a girl came over and said, "Mr Nevinson? Your taxi is here." I thought there must be a mistake, but glancing through the windows, recognised our own Father Christmas.

I went to fetch the coats, and the tree-stand had turned into a forest. Each of the ten arms had three or four coats on, mostly black, hanging there like a colony of bats, and with great difficulty I extricated ours. Greeted effusively by Danny, we tottered over to the cab, and I climbed in, already feeling that I had eaten too much - so much so that I didn't want to button up the coat over a straining middle!

There was much banter with Danny before he dropped us at Mum's bungalow. We walked up the path, laughing that there was no washing-up to do - it was going to be such an easy afternoon this year. It was when I announced that I was feeling quite happily dozy and would go back to my house and have a lie-down that Mum said, "What's that on your coat?"

I looked down. It was the most beautiful large expensive silver brooch.

"You've got the wrong coat!" said Mum, quicker off the mark than me, who wondered why this mysterious brooch had attached itself to my smart new short black coat.

No chance of a post-prandial lie-down now!

"Sorry to bother you," I said, as the phone at the hotel was picked up.

"Yes?" replied a tinny voice on the telephone.

"I have just arrived home from Christmas dinner with you, and I'm afraid I've picked up the wrong coat."

Gosh, it sounded so stupid. The voice went to fetch the deputy manager.

"Hello? This is Philip. You have the wrong coat, sir?"

"Yes," I said lamely.

"And I have a very upset lady here…" he began.

"I'm sorry," I interrupted, "but I came out by taxi, and it'll be impossible to book another one now on Christmas afternoon, so if you just give me the lady's name and telephone number then I'll sort things out with her, and try to get the coat returned."

There was the briefest pause and Philip said, "Don't worry. I'll be at your house in the next twenty minutes and pick up the coat."

I started to tell him that was more than kind, but the line went dead. Half an hour later, I had my coat returned, and the Brooch Lady would soon have hers back.

"Didn't you notice the different buttoning?" asked Mum, after singing the praises of the deputy manager.

"When I fell into that taxi, I felt too stuffed to think of fastening it," I explained. And so awake now that there was no thought of having a snooze!

The following Christmas it was easy to persuade my visiting sister and her husband that a Christmas dinner at that same hotel would be a good idea. No major shopping. No sorting out Brussel sprouts on Christmas Eve. No working out pounds and ounces and minutes for the turkey. No getting up at an unearthly hour to put the oven on. No letting the Christmas pudding dry out. No washing up. No days of plundering the bony carcase to create turkey salad, turkey risotto, turkey and chips, turkey soup…

We dutifully dressed up and travelled in their car down the Eden Valley...

As we walked into the hotel, a passing waiter directed us to a hatch where an attractive young girl sat with an assortment of buff-coloured cloakroom tickets in front of her. She smiled as she looked up, and said, "If you can take a ticket, I will check in your coats."

"Oh, that's a new idea," I smiled.

She wrinkled her nose.

"Well, it's necessary - last year some stupid man walked off with the wrong coat."

There was half a second's hush before I heard the laughter.

"It was him! It was *him!*" Pointing at me, my brother-in-law was grinning from ear to ear, as were my sister and mother.

So now, if I go out for a meal with them, or anybody else who has been regaled with the infamous tale of the stolen coat, I can be sure that, as it is time to go home, some wit in the party will say, "Now just check carefully, John. Are you sure you've got the right coat? No nice silver brooch?"

The Bone Of Contention

Karl knew that he had a major mistake in coming to Glasgow as soon as he left Central Station. He looked at the long line of black taxis on Hope Street; an auburn-haired girl was leaning in the window of one, chatting to a Pakistani driver, and as she glanced up and smiled at Karl, he realised how much she looked like Laurie. But then, didn't *all* women? Ever since Laurie had walked out on him and gone back home to her mother, Karl saw her smile, her hair, her eyes, her walk in every woman who passed him. He looked at his watch, and saw that they were not due to meet for another hour, so he decided to saunter through the city centre, and collect his confused thoughts about Laurie, Roger and himself.

Karl soon found himself walking up Buchanan Street, the pedestrianised pavement crowded with Saturday morning shoppers; an early rain shower had gone, and the grey paving flags dazzled his eyes in the harsh low November sunshine. Everywhere he looked, Karl was reminded of the moments of his shared history with Laurie - the high-class Jermyn Street gents' outfitters where she bought him an expensive birthday tie, the jewellers where they had looked at engagement rings, the Willow Tea Rooms where she had enthused about the Rennie Mackintosh design...

Soon, too soon, Karl had climbed the slight hill and reached the top end of Buchanan Street; he thought about a coffee at the Concert Hall, but changed his mind when he realised that soon he would be having one with his estranged wife. He managed to avoid stepping on a bobble-hatted figure, sitting splay-legged on the damp pavement with a polystyrene-cup begging bowl and a mangy Jack Russell on a string, and turned into Sauchiehall Street. And more memories of his times in Glasgow with Laurie flooded back - the huge Waterstones bookshop where they had browsed contentedly for hours, another bigger and grander Willow Tea room, the silly present bought for Roger at the Danish novelty shop, the big Primark where she replaced the gloves she had left at the Modern Art Museum...

And now Karl was on his way to meet Laurie at another museum. Glancing at his watch, he speeded up a little, made his way along a dingier section of bars and kebab shops on Sauchiehall Street, over the continuous roar of traffic going into the underpass, and past terraces of classy well-maintained nineteenth-century houses. At last, the Kelvingrove Museum and Art Gallery appeared, a gigantic sandstone mixture of Spanish baroque and Victorian Gothic. Karl felt his nervous stomach tighten as he made his way up the steps and through the revolving glass doors into the museum.

As usual, Karl's breath was taken away as he entered the enormous main hall, with its huge vaulted ceiling. An organ recital was taking place, with rows of chairs facing the battery of pipes and the illuminated box below them where the musician played. At eye-level, two television screens showed the details of hands straying over the keyboard and feet dancing over the pedals. Karl was just thinking how amazing the footwork was, and about the incredible dexterity needed to juggle hands and feet when a gentle voice said, "Hello, Karl." He spun around, and Laurie was smiling at him. Before he could speak or decide whether it was right or not to hug her, she said, "The tea shop over there is pretty basic, Karl. The one is the basement is so much better," and set off towards the steps. At the foot, they turned past the glowing invitation of the gift shop, and entered the café. A slim girl with an Italian accent led them to a table on an outer section, right up against large windows that looked over the River Kelvin to woodland which surrounded the Gothic University buildings.

"Well..." began Laurie, and she put out her hand and squeezed Karl's wrist.

"Here we are," he added, huskily as he hadn't spoken since he'd bought a drink on the train.

"Your Mum and Dad OK?" she asked.

"Fine, thanks. And Senga?"

"Mum's fine, thanks."

Pleasantries over, a kind of civility between them confirmed, silence descended. Before it became too strained, the Italian girl came for their order, so they scanned the menu and decided on scones, jam and tea.

"Job going well?" asked Karl.

"Fine, thanks," replied Laurie. "It's a bit of a hike to Falkirk each day, but the trains are good, and the school isn't that far from the station."

"You don't fancy moving to Falkirk?"

"No, Karl. Mum loves having me back home at Newton Mearns, and I'm enjoying the attention! And anyway, I love Glasgow too much. My native city. I hadn't realised just how much I missed the dear green place."

"Dear green place?" scoffed Karl.

"Och, yes," retorted Laurie, slightly irritated by her husband's flippancy. "Grannie Macfadzean always told me that Glasgow meant 'dear green place' in Gaelic."

There was the start of an awkward silence, and then the Italian girl arrived with the tea tray. Laurie picked up the heavy white teapot, and poured an exploratory dribble into her cup before shaking her head, and putting the pot down. Karl cut his scone in two, and tried to spread on the pack of butter which was still frozen from the fridge, with the result that the yellow rectangle lay there solid and unyielding.

"And things going OK for you at work in Carlisle?" asked Laurie.

"Yes, thanks. Solicitors are always busy."

Subconsciously, the couple knew that any possible discussion was foundering on the chit-chat about jobs and parents because hovering above them was the subject which was hard to mention. They buttered scones, sipped tea and let their minds race over the unspoken conversation until Laurie bit the bullet.

"So, the elephant in the room…" she started.

"The elephant, Laurie?"

"Roger," she said, and stared directly at him.

Karl shifted uncomfortably in his chair, as Laurie buttered a scone purposefully, and took a large bite from it to force her necessary silence and Karl's requested response.

"Not exactly an elephant, is he? Roger? He's fine, thanks," said Karl at last.

"Good. I knew he wasn't so well at one stage," she said.

"No, the poor chap got over that intestinal problem. Lot of discomfort at the time."

"Time. Hmm. It was the amount of time you spent with Roger that…" Laurie couldn't finish the sentence as her eyes welled up, and she flapped her fingers in a fan-like theatrical gesture in front of them. Karl put down the butter knife, and stared at her, thinking, "Here we go again. I *knew* this would happen. Histrionics. She goes from zero to top speed in seconds. She was the one who upped and left for Glasgow, saying she was fed up with the amount of time I devoted to Roger. How ridiculous! This time...*this* time, we will have it out!"

Laurie finished her performance, dabbed her mouth with the paper napkin and returned to the sentence which she had been unable to complete.

"You spent all your time with him," she wailed. "I would want to go out somewhere, and you would start saying that Roger..."

"Oh, for God's sake, Laurie," interrupted Karl. "Don't try to sound like the poor neglected wife. You liked Roger very much at first..."

"At first!" she cut in. "At *first!*"

"I know Roger could be demanding..."

"*Demanding!*" shrilled Laurie, and an elderly couple stared over, and then turned back to their teacups whispering. "There were nights when I never saw you at all. In from work, quick dinner, and then off out with bloody Roger for the rest of the evening."

"Stop exaggerating, Laurie..." he began.

"I might just as well had been a widow, for all the evenings I sat alone watching tv, while you two were out having fun," she wailed.

"Yes, I'll admit that I spent many of my evenings with Roger. Nearly every night..."

"*Every* night! And I *didn't* ever see you at weekends. At one point I even wondered if you really were out with Roger. I began to think that you had another woman!"

Karl began to laugh which upset his wife even more.

"Why would I want somebody else when I had the best-looking woman in Carlisle?" he asked.

"Well, Karl, obviously that wasn't enough for you. *I* wasn't enough for you! All *you* wanted was bloody

Roger!" Laurie was sobbing now, and the elderly couple shuffled a quick embarrassed exit from their uncomfortable ringside table.

"For Pete's sake, Laurie!" hissed Karl.

"No! I am right. And I think... I think... I really think that Roger was the love of your life!"

Karl shook his head in disbelief as the tears coursed down Laurie's cheeks. This was a replay of the evening seven months ago when, out of the blue, Laurie told him she was applying for a job in Scotland, and going home to her mother. He had thought that his wife's stupid and unreasonable jealousy about his relationship with Roger would have evaporated away, but it seemed to be stronger than ever. Why was Laurie so angry about Roger? She was his wife, and he loved her. Well, he *had* loved her, but watching this tear-streaked gibbering harpy loudly berating him in a museum tea room... It had knocked any hopes he might have had about some kind of reconciliation. As far as he was concerned Laurie could damn well stay with her Mum in Newton Mearns, and commute daily to Falkirk till hell froze over. It was finished. Karl stood up.

"That's right! Leave me. Leave me again!" she shouted.

"Again? Don't be such a drama queen! When did I ever leave you, Laurie?" he snapped.

"That night I had the bleeding from the wisdom tooth extraction. I was in agony. And you.... You had planned to go to London for the weekend with bloody Roger! And so off you both gaily went, without a single thought for me," she sobbed.

"That visit had been planned for a long time, and we just *had* to go to London..." Karl reasoned.

"Why? *Why?* Why did you both have to go to London that weekend, and leave me? What was so important?"

Karl was aware now that the two waitresses and the counter staff had stopped work, and, like the few customers who had heard Laurie's loud comments about Roger being the love of Karl's life, they were transfixed by these unexpected theatrics in the Kelvingrove Museum restaurant.

"What was so important?" shouted Karl, throwing Laurie's question back at her. "What was so flaming important?"

"Yes!" she screeched. "Why did you leave me and go to London for that weekend with Roger?"

"Because I thought I might be on to a winner that weekend," said Karl, flinging the words down the restaurant as he strode out, fervently hoping never to see Laurie again. "I hoped that Roger would win the Best Border Collie section at bloody Crufts!"

This originally appeared in my collection of short stories Nothing Can Possibly Go Wrong!

Janette Fisher

Janette is a 57-year-old mother with two grown-up daughters She works full-time as the Administration and Finance Officer for a charitable project which provides training and support for adults with learning disabilities.

She has been writing since school and has had several poems published, in four anthologies by Forward Press and *The People's Friend*. In 2013, her poem 'Music and Memories' came fourth in the *National Association of Writers' Group*'s Formal Poetry competition. Janette's first collection of poetry, *There's Enough Blue in the Sky* was published in 2015 by Lapwing and she is currently working on her second.

Notes On Life

Through the years, I've known my share of sorrow,
Had my life shattered by cancer and death,
With days, when I couldn't face tomorrow

And dark endless nights, when feeling bereft
I've cried a thousand tears. They fell like rain,
Again, and again, until nothing was left

But silent screams, piercing through the pain
Deep inside my heart. There were times, I thought
The pain would never end, and griefs refrain

The only tune I'd sing, until I sought
Solace in poetry, music and song,
Finding the peace and contentment it brought

A refuge. My haven, in a choir's throng
And time with reflections, paper and pen,
Was medication needed to grow strong

In order to move forward – live again.
Words and music stayed, when all else was gone
And played a new melody. It was then,
I found a voice, to walk once more in the sun.

Locked-In

"How are you feeling today?"

"Trapped."

They don't hear
and set about their tasks
with constant moans:
this and that,
idle chat.
I can't bear their drones
"Enough!"

They don't hear,
don't care:
I'm locked in this shell
awake, aware,
paralysed,
unable to move or talk
since the pain
burned through my head.

I lie in this bed
wired to a fear-filled machine.
Moments clicked
a switch flicked,
my locked-in scream...
"Don't do it. Please.
I'm still here!"

"How are you today?"

The Trouble With Brothers!

Looking back over my childhood, whenever I found myself holding the short end of the 'troubles stick,' it usually involved my older brother. Three years my elder, John and I were almost inseparable. He was Bootsie to my Snudge; Laurel to my Hardy; Tom to my Jerry. Wherever he went, I went (not always by invitation) which inevitably led me, if not both of us, into trouble.

The earliest memory I recall, was when I was about three years old, coming down the stairs of our small council house on a lovely summer's morning, the smell of yeast permeating the air as mum made bread for the day. Our sister Lyn, just newly born, was fast asleep in her pram outside the back door where mum could keep an eye on her, and John was out in the garden, blissfully at play in the sun. I plainly remember feeling the excitement of wanting, and needing, to be out playing beside him, and it took all the strength mum had to brush my hair and tie me down to the breakfast table to eat, before letting me out of the door to join him. We played in the sun for hours that day, the first time I truly felt the love of family. It was the start of many happy times we'd spend together over our childhood years as a duo. Today, the smell of fresh bread baking always takes me back to that day and fills me with nostalgia and love.

Looking back, it was a time similar to that of Enid Blyton's 'Famous Five.' We were naive and unworldly, and I often wish I could turn back the clock to those times, when both of our parents were still here and our age of innocence was just beginning. We played outside from morn until night without thought of evil in the world and had many an adventure. These were the best of times. I'm not saying some of our adventures didn't go awry, because they did, and there were occasions when we did stupid things when we really should have known better.

Take 'The Incident of the Red Shoe,' as John and I call it. It was Easter time 1967. Back in those days, parents would put aside money from their hard- earned wages, to provide their children with new clothes to wear to church on Easter Sunday morning, before visiting relatives to receive chocolate eggs, pasche eggs and oranges. Our parents didn't have a lot of spare cash to splash about (Mum had two part-time jobs and Dad was a bus driver) so the clothes we wore at Easter would be our 'Sunday Best' for the coming year. We had to look after them! This particular Easter, my outfit included a new pair of red patent leather, slip-on shoes with a big silver buckle on the front and I felt like Dorothy from *The Wizard of Oz* when I wore them, polishing them every day, army-style, like dad had taught me until I could see my face reflected in them.

In the weeks prior to that Easter, it had rained constantly and the fields where we played close to home were muddy and boggy, so Mum had warned us to wear our playing-out shoes whenever we went out. Beside the playing fields, the council were building a new connecting road between the two major routes into the city as the old one couldn't cope with the amount of traffic using it. The work-site had lots of giant concrete sewage pipes standing waiting to be laid when the builders came back after the Bank Holiday. While the workmen had been away, the pipes had become a playground for all the estate kids.

On this particular morning, I saw John running out of the house, heading toward the site to play. Feeling left out, I was keen to follow him, so I picked up the first pair of shoes I could lay my hands on, which happened to be my Dorothy ones, and headed out into the muggy, damp morning.

It didn't take long for me to regret leaving the house. We'd been playing for about half an hour, running in and out of the pipes, chasing each other and our cousins, who had joined us, when my feet got stuck in a particularly boggy bit of ground. I pulled hard, managing to get my left foot out, but the right one had gone too far down. With the mud as soft as quicksand, the more I struggled to get it out, the deeper my foot went until I screamed hysterically for John and the others to come and help. Using pieces of wood lying about as spades, John and my cousins dug desperately until my right leg was finally free, but when it came out, there was no shoe. The swamp had swallowed it into a muddy grave. Terrified of leaving without it, we continued digging for about another hour without a trace.

I didn't know how I was going to tell my parents and wished I could be like Dorothy and click the red shoes together to go back in time. I knew this was going to entail a harsh punishment, and how right I was! I received a hiding from my father, was grounded for a month and lost pocket money privileges to pay for a new pair of shoes. It took weeks of no Saturday morning cinema or watching Carlisle play football until there was enough money for replacement shoes. You can be assured I never, ever, again wore them when I went out to play. John and I went back to the worksite every day for weeks to see if the workmen had found the missing shoe but it had totally disappeared and was never seen again. I learned a hard lesson that day, and the surviving Dorothy shoe sat on a cushion in my room for years, as a reminder.

Of course, this wasn't the only incident involving us both. There were many over the years; like the time I was grounded for coming home late from the disco. I snuck out of my bedroom window to see my best friend; coming home an hour later, I found that John had closed the window so I couldn't sneak back in. I had to knock on the front door, only to face the wrath of my mother and get grounded for a further week.

Or the time we were left in charge of Dad's car at Maryport harbour while everyone else had a look around the town. We accidentally locked the keys in the boot, so we had to take out the back seats and I had to climb through the back of the boot to retrieve them.

On another occasion, John tried to cheer me up after I'd broken up with my boyfriend, by taking me for a walk. We started out on a sunny afternoon, only intending to be out for an hour, but somewhere along the way we took a wrong turn, ending up half way to Penrith, when the weather changed. We returned home to worried parents five hours later - cold, sopping wet and hungry.

Then there was the time John got run over by a motorbike as we played British Bulldogs in the street; the time he took me out in dad's car to teach me to drive and we crashed in to a ditch; the time we got extremely drunk on a night out and slept under the railway embankment… and many more besides. We both remember them fondly and laugh about them when we meet.

Looking back, I can state with some certainty that, yes, when trouble found me, it was usually with John but as Yin has Yang, when adversity also found me, John was there too. He was there during my abusive first marriage and the first person at my door when I finally walked away from it. He travelled hundreds of miles to be with me when both our parents died and helped organise everything. He has been the one constant in my life; my sanity, when my beloved husband was diagnosed with cancer, standing beside me holding my hand when Billy took his final breath and giving his eulogy. John has supported me through the darkest of days since.

Throughout the years, I haven't regretted any of our adventures as they made us who we are today and I've loved every minute. In this, John's sixtieth, we're as close as ever, so I'm planning a special adventure to celebrate, because I want him to know how much I appreciate him being there for me, through the good and the bad, because the trouble with brothers is – you love them unconditionally and simply can't live without them.

Janet Patrick

Janet was born and brought up in Carlisle and over the years has worked in many different places, including offices, schools and factories. She loves nature, walking and drawing. She finds writing a way to create pictures with words that lead to telling stories.

Janet first came to the Writers' Group in June 2014 and enjoyed the experience of sharing work in a friendly, encouraging atmosphere.

Blue Belladonna

Blue Belladonna, my Belladonna blue,
A dream and a nightmare are blended in you.
Catching my stare with a piercing gaze
Your eyes in a crowd stayed with me for days.

Blue Belladonna, my Belladonna blue,
The first time I saw you I felt that I knew
Your face from a memory hidden by cloud
Your voice, though I never had heard it out loud.

Blue Belladonna, my Belladonna blue,
A spell you have cast and it draws me to you.
A draught in a goblet you offer to me,
Tastes of your perfume, I'll never be free.

Daffodil

A slender reed of green,
Resting between my fingers,
A shaft of hope
Glimpsed from the swirling torrent
Closing above my head,
A wand of potency
Cast into the water,
You call me
With whispered words of spring.
A dream of yellow
Breaks into daylight.

Moment

Soft, dove grey blends to ochre.
Raw stillness hints at snow.
A distant ticking of a clock.
Lost in thought as thought falls away.

A drift, a shift, a slide,
Side stepping without a step,
Held by nothing, holding nothing,
Being, as ever being.

Jacqui Issatt

Jacqui grew up in Appleby and has lived and worked in Carlisle for almost twenty years. She has always been a keen reader and whilst studying for a degree in Literature with the Open University, a friend suggested she try writing fiction.

Jacqui likes reading stories by new writers and tries to support the small independent presses that publish them. She enjoys reading short story collections and new writers' debut novels.

First joining CWG in 2010, Jacqui took a break to complete her degree before returning in 2016. She finds being part of the group helpful as it gives her writing a purpose, as well as the chance to hear other people's work.

A Winter's Meeting

The rising warm air is cosy, soothing, but Zoe's synapses remain fully engaged on containing the creatures. So concentrated is she on the swarm that she does not fully hear what the voice overhead is saying. She shifts her concentration and, raising her head from the window pane. she reads the sign: Skipton. Only about half an hour to go. The butterflies surge from her stomach into her chest; she breathes deeply to push them back down.

The Agency had recommended their first meeting should a brief, daytime one, nothing too full on, just a chance to introduce themselves, see what they think. If they want to carry on from there, they can, but neither of them would be under any obligation to do so. So, they had agreed to meet at the station and go for lunch, just a couple of hours. Leeds is closer for him, but that suits her; she won't bring him back to Carlisle until she is sure.

As the train pulls forward again, Zoe returns her head to the window pane, letting her eyelids droop. The air coming from the heaters is stuffy now. Sitting up, she picks her copy of *Bridget Jones' Diary* off the table once more and opens it. Her eyes can see the text on the page but her brain cannot decipher it. For over a week, words have been beyond her. What will she say to him? "Hello." Then what? "Paul." "Hello, Paul." It doesn't feel right in her mouth his name; she has no claim on it yet. The Agency advised keeping the conversation light, nothing too personal or deep in the beginning. Stringing a sentence together or thinking of a question to ask him enlivens the butterflies, their beating wings batting any thoughts from her mind.

Replacing the book on the table, Zoe stares at the cover; she wouldn't have picked it herself, but most of the women at her book club had been keen to read it so this is their book for the month. What will Paul think if he sees it? Zoe doesn't want to give the wrong impression; she is a serious woman with interests, opinions and not a lover of 'chick-lit.' She goes to the bathroom to check her make-up and re-apply her lipstick. Returning to her seat, she smooths down the brown wraparound dress to stop it creasing across her thighs. Is this too formal, too work-like? Would jeans and a jumper have been better? The train is slowing again.

In his last message he'd said he was really looking forward to meeting her, though he admitted he was nervous, which had made her feel better, bold even. But now... she was the one who had asked to meet. Their messages weren't enough; she wants to hear his voice, see his facial expressions, to smell his smell. Imagination has made all those things and more, familiar. She has pictured holidays - lying on the sand, swimming in the sea together, him leading them around beautiful coral reefs. Weekend walks in Gelt Woods, and after, she'll cook them a roast, which he will love, then they'll watch a film together. Often in those dreams, his arm is around her shoulders, pulling her towards him, always laughing, joyful, natural.

The turning wheels continue to pull the train along the tracks. Odd houses in the countryside become clusters, become streets; eventually the cityscape is established in the moving picture frame of the window. Zoe scoops her things into her bag and heads for the door. Anticipating the cold outside, she pulls the hood of her duffle-coat under her chin. The sun is shining in the clear, powder-blue sky, but even as it approaches its zenith, she knows it is not powerful enough to warm the January air. As the door slides open she inhales deeply, filling her lungs and holding the air for a second before letting it burst from her.

Dropping down on to the platform, the kaleidoscope of passengers begins to move towards the exit. After a few steps Zoe feels as though she is being pushed forward like the crest of a breaking wave. Looking around, she spots a seating area at the end of the platform. Picking her way through the crowd to the row of red plastic chairs, she perches herself on the edge of the least grimy one. Fumbling fingers trawl the handbag for cigarettes. "God, why do I keep so much stuff in here?" Removing the book from her bag to get a better look inside, she finds him staring up at her. In his picture she sees brown hair almost as dark as hers, but he has an attractive salt and pepper sprinkling of grey around the ears. His broad smile and warm, hazel-coloured eyes give him an air of kindness.

The first few draughts on the cigarette relax her briefly, though the butterflies remain poised. What is she doing here? They have only exchanged a few emails after the Agency put them in touch. Maybe this is a bad idea. It's too soon. Turning to put her cigarette out in the ashtray, she sees him; actual, real him, in a navy suit, holding a bunch of tulips, walking into the station. She stands up but her feet do not know whether to run to or from him, so they remain still. It seems as if he can feel where she is, for although he has not seen her, he is walking right towards her.

Paul stops to check his watch and adjust his tie, then looking up again he sees her. His eyes expand. Each step he takes broadens his smile a little further. Now here he is right in front of her. It is all she can do to breathe.

"Hello, Zoe."

"Hello... Dad. I can't believe it's you, it's been so long."

He opens his arms towards her, she steps forward, and for the first time in twenty-seven years, he holds her close to him, the squeeze of his arms setting the butterflies free.

Secret Symphony

Leaning against the front seat, Steven waited for the bus to stop. Stepping out on to the pavement, he was engulfed once again by the thick, motionless air of an early June heat wave. Pearls of sweat popped out of every pore, his stomach fizzed with hunger. He put his hands in his trouser pockets: twelve pence, some fluff, and a bent paper-clip. He'd have to wait until he got home. Would the letter have arrived today? No, Mum would have texted him to say if it

152

had. He turned left at the sun-bed shop on Smithfield Avenue. It was so humid even the shade of the trees lining the road offered no respite.

As he plodded along, his thoughts moved from food to homework. The maths exercises would only take him quarter of an hour, the history essay could wait until the weekend; it was too hot to think. Bending his right elbow and pulling his arm back, he slid his hand into the side pocket of his school bag. His fingers searched for and found his mobile phone. He pulled it out of his pocket, connected the earphones and switched on the radio. He tried Radio 3 where they were discussing Wagner. He switched to Classic FM. Ahh, Tchaikovsky's *Violin Concerto in D Major.*

Steven paused at the corner of Lichfield Road, his own street. Rows of bay-windowed terraced houses with small, walled front gardens lined either side of the steep hill. Steven and his Mum lived in number one, on the right-hand side, at the top. Their house was separated from the others by the path leading to the park and pond, behind their back yard. His nose slowly drew in two lungfuls of flaccid air. Releasing it, he started his slow trudge. The concerto had come to the third movement. Steven tried to make his mind's eye see the position of the violinist's fingers on the neck, the speed of the bow and the pressure needed on the strings.

'Beep, Beep!' The text message tone jolted him out of his study. He fished the phone out of his trouser pocket and looked at the screen. It was 'Hank' - Andrew Hancock-wanting to know if he was coming to the disco at the Youth Club on Friday night, and was he going to chip in to get some bottles of *Strongbow* with the other lads? Steven slipped the phone back into his pocket. Looking up, he was surprised to see that he was already at the top of the hill where it levelled out.

Dropping his bag on the bottom stair, Steven went into the kitchen. He opened the fridge door. The cool air emitted was lovely, chilling the pearls on his skin, giving him goose-pimples. He stared at the full shelves for a few seconds, before picking up the cheese-spread. As he waited for the toaster to do its work, he heard someone moving in the sitting room.

"Stevie, is that you?" his Mum called.

"Yeah." Ping! His two slices of nearly burnt toast were ready. He trowelled the spread on to one piece and took two large bites from it before smothering the second. Mum appeared in the doorway, hands behind her back. Her blonde, curly hair was squashed flat on her left side, which Steven knew meant she had been asleep on the sofa

"This came for you today," she said holding out a small white envelope. Steven took it from her, seeing the local Bury postmark across the top. His heart made two beats in the space of one.

He walked over to the table beside the back-door, pulled out one of the chairs and wilted on to it. He placed the envelope on the table and stuffed half of the second slice of toast into his mouth. Mum came and sat on the chair next to him. As he lifted his hand to his mouth again, he glanced sideways at her. Greenish-blue eyes bore into him like the sun's ray through a magnifying glass, the fabric of her slightly too-tight pink vest top jumped up and down over her cleavage in time with her breath. Finishing his food, Steven picked up the envelope with both hands and looked at it.

"Aren't you going to open it?" Mum asked. He said nothing, just kept on looking at the envelope.

"Look, if you don't get it this time, you can always try again," she almost whispered. He didn't want to try again: he wanted *this* to be it.

There had been three interviewers at the second exam; two women and a man. He couldn't remember their names. He'd been so nervous, he'd dropped the bow as he lifted it to start playing, which he'd thought strange, because he knew the piece so well. Mendelssohn's *Violin Concerto in E Minor* was the first piece of violin music Steven could remember listening to. The sound clarity of the violin had resonated in him to such a degree that it felt as though each atom within him vibrated at the same frequency as the string playing the note.

Sitting up in the chair, Steven inhaled deeply and shoved his thumb under the flap at the back of the envelope. He took out the piece of paper and his eyes saw what he already knew: the letter was headed with the logo of *Bury Youth Orchestra*. Slowly, he unfolded the letter: 'Dear Steven Jackson, We are delighted to be able to offer you a place...' He opened his mouth but no words came out.

"Well?" Mum's voice cracked. He held out the letter and her eyes quickly darted over the first couple of lines.

"Oh, Stevie, well done!" She stood up and poured herself on top of him. One arm around his neck, the other under his arm; she pressed him to her so tightly he couldn't get any air.

Steven stayed at the kitchen table, holding the letter and staring out of the window into the back yard. He watched the sweet-peas wrapped around the trellis on the back wall sway, conducted by the shimmering hot air. Mum flitted about the kitchen like a sparrow making a nest. She was going to cook his favourite dinner; baked macaroni cheese with tuna. All the while she was gathering the ingredients and grating the cheese, she chattered away, a symphony of satisfaction and pride, but Steven only heard Tchaikovsky's concerto playing in his mind's ear. It took him a second or two to notice that she had stopped speaking.

"What?" he asked, finally taking his eyes off the flowers.

"Aren't you going to let your friends at school know the good news?" she beamed.

I Haven't A Clue

I haven't a clue how long this valley is,
Or where it leads to.
I haven't a clue what flowers are blooming on the hill side,
I haven't a clue.

I haven't a clue how many miles we've walked,
Or how many there are left to go.
I haven't a clue when this quest will end,
I haven't a clue.

I haven't a clue where we'll sleep tonight,
If we'll be out under star-light.
I haven't a clue if wolves live in those woods,
I haven't a clue.

I haven't a clue when I'll next be in school,
Or what tongue the pupils will use.
I haven't a clue if the teacher will be kind or stern,
I haven't a clue.

I haven't a clue if our house remains as one solid piece,
Or has been pulverised to dust.
I haven't a clue if our apricot tree blossomed this year,
I haven't a clue.

I haven't a clue when the night will come that mother does
not weep,
Or when father's laugh will bubble up and out again.
I haven't a clue how long the blisters on my feet will take
to heal,
I haven't a clue.

I haven't a clue if uncle Ismail and aunt Nadia were able to
get on a boat,
Or if they wait on a turning tide,
I haven't a clue how they'd find us now.
I haven't a clue.

I haven't a clue why a bomb was dropped on our street,
Or how many of our neighbours died.
I haven't a clue how those who stay on survive,
I haven't a clue.

I haven't a clue, when all are done who will be declared
the victor,
Or what triumph will look like.
I haven't a clue if the phoenix will make home in my land,

Ella Atherton

Former front-line social worker/practice teacher/senior practitioner and team manager in Children's Services, Ella thinks she has gathered enough material to fill several books, starting with three items in this anthology, none of which (she promises) are based on real people.

Ella read psychology, sociology and social policy at Lancaster University; subjects that continue to fascinate her and seem to find their way into her writings. A life-long avid reader, a lover and collector of books, she is a recent convert to not-too-gory crime fiction.

It Must Have Happened On The Train

Rich thought her the most beautiful girl he'd ever seen. From her oval face framed in delicious tendrils of natural blonde hair to her purple painted toenails caressed by matching-coloured sandals, he considered her a vision of Cumbrian chic.

"Dizzy blonde, probably thick," he said, indicating the girl in the adjacent seat in carriage D on the 9.25 TransPennine Express tippity-tappiting its way from Carlisle Citadel to the Macron Stadium in Bolton.

"She doesn't need a brain for what you have in mind," mocked Mike as they supped Jenning's *Cockahoop* from plastic beakers that still held the memory of railway coffee.

"Give over. I haven't got time for women. Too much bevy to neck," responded Rich, saluting Mike with his coffee cup.

The two friends chatted about the forthcoming match,

dissecting Bolton Wanderers' recent demotion and Carlisle's diminishing chances. They could hear ex-pat Boltonians chanting two carriages away. The buffet car separated the opposing supporters so Mike volunteered to get them both a bacon sandwich. During his absence, Rich couldn't keep his eyes off the girl. She sensed his gaze, returned eye contact and smiled. Rich, with alcohol-filled confidence, took it as an invitation. Vacating his window seat, he joined the girl across the aisle. She didn't object and Rich discovered her name was Laura and she wasn't thick at all. She was a recent Manchester University law graduate and on her way to a job interview at the law firm Bibby & Patel in Lancaster. Rich offered Laura some of his hidden *Cockahoop* and to his surprise, she accepted. They were deep in conversation when Mike returned. He took the hint and sat in his old seat to eat both sandwiches alone.

Laura and Rich took the opportunity for a more private tête-a-tête when they saw the ticket collector sway his way through their carriage, leaving his work booth unattended...

Things got surprisingly passionate in the booth. Rich couldn't believe his luck and Laura couldn't believe how easily she had thrown caution to the wind. All too soon the train approached Lancaster. They hurriedly adjusted their clothing and agreed to meet on the return journey.

Carlisle were beaten 2-1, but Rich's disappointment was off-set by the thought of seeing Laura again. To his dismay, the train failed to stop at Lancaster. Rich could have kicked himself for not exchanging mobile numbers with Laura when he had the chance.

Back in Carlisle, Rich tried to trace Laura through Facebook and Google. He even checked Manchester University's year book and local electoral registers:

nothing. He looked out for her in Carlisle and thought about her often.

Over a year later, Rich spotted Laura walking past Carlisle's Old Town Hall. She was pushing a child's buggy. He ran up to her and when he looked in the buggy his mini-me looked back at him. There was no mistaking those brown eyes, curly black hair, ebony skin and lady-killer smile. Rich was rooted to the spot, mind whirring, heart racing. He looked at Laura; the big question in his eyes. Laura made a shushing sound when a white man with light brown hair bounded over and planted a kiss on her cheek.

"This is my husband," she said. "He's a senior partner at Bibby's."

Fish Swap

Lorraine reckoned it must have been her painted toe-nails that attracted the little fish, sending them into a frenzy that exceeded their remit of just nibbling the dead skin off customers' feet. Instead they tore pulsating strips of living flesh from Lorraine's big toe, exposing the bone with such speed, she barely had time to scream as she leapt off the bench into the arms of a male attendant. Two other customers who had been sitting either side of Lorraine joined in the screaming that reached a crescendo when they saw the tank fill with blood. An off-duty nurse had the presence of mind to encase Lorraine's once-elegant foot in a plastic bag while the attendant closed the blinds (much to the annoyance of a crowd of curious on-lookers attracted by the screaming).

Bedlam ensued in the shop as other customers joined in

the screaming. Only the nurse had the prescience to call an ambulance, which arrived at the shopping centre within fifteen minutes (according to the police report afterwards). The paramedics applied non-stick wound pads to Lorraine's foot and offered her gas and air to dull the pain. The younger of the two paramedics searched the fish tank to see if he could find enough of Lorraine's toe to make reconstruction viable. He put his gloved hand into the tank. The fish immediately attacked the latex, sensing meat beneath. The paramedic swiftly withdrew his hand, latex shredded but digits still intact.

"All present and correct," he stated, holding his hand aloft as he counted his fingers. He could see through the swirling blood in the tank that there was nothing left of Lorraine's flesh. All that remained was a single silver-painted toe nail at the bottom of the tank. The fish ignored the nail as they continued to swarm back and forth in their lethal hunting shoal.

"Sorry," said the paramedic, "Nothing worth rescuing."

Hearing this news, Lorraine burst into tears, tears that threatened to fill the plastic mask covering her nose and mouth. Her sobs were mixed with coughs, splutters and insane laughter as the nitrous oxide, better known as laughing gas, did its pain-reducing work.

"My toe, my toe," cried Lorraine, "it hurts like billy-o. Ha, ha. Billy-o, big toe. Oh, it hurts."

"Come on, lass," said the older of the two paramedics. "Take another deep breath. You'll be all right."

"Did you see that?" said one customer to another as they waited in line for their turn in *Pedi-Spa*. "The fish have eaten her feet. Come on. Let's get out of here."

The attendant, wearing a white, clinical-looking jacket with *Pedi-Spa* emblazoned in red script on his lapel, tried to calm the customers who had already paid, those who hadn't had managed to bolt out of the door. The attendant rushed to lock the door to stop the other customers fleeing and prevent rubber-neckers pouring into the treatment area. But first, he ordered the man taking pictures to leave.

"You! Out immediately!" he ordered as he bundled the photographer out the door.

"I thought those fish were harmless," cried Lorraine through gulps of gas and air.

"More like bloody piranha," said one of the women who'd been sitting next to her on the bench. "I read in *The Sun* that chin chin are often mistaken for nibbler fish. Chin chin grow teeth when they get older. I bet those *Pedi* buggers swapped them without knowing the difference." Lorraine began to cry again. "Don't worry, lass," she soothed, "You'll be all right."

The ambulance blue-lighted its way through the congested streets of Carlisle but still managed to arrive at the Cumberland Infirmary within fourteen minutes (according to the same police report). As the paramedic had surmised, there wasn't enough flesh left to reconstruct Lorraine's toe. "Nor time to grow extra," said the receiving registrar, 'or graft flesh from the patient's belly, which is the flattest I've ever seen."

"Well, I've never seen such a clean wound either," said the surgeon to the registrar, as he stood back to allow the theatre nurse to dress what remained of Lorraine's mutilated hallux.

"The patient can stay overnight. Discharge her tomorrow if there's no infection."

While Lorraine was being operated on, the *Pedi-Spa* organisation went into overdrive as they tried to limit the fallout from bad publicity and plug any loopholes that might hold them liable for compensation. The chief executive, Donald Sucre, struggling to hold his temper, ordered his PR people to issue bulletins to all news agencies, pointing out that the Health Protection Agency (HPA) had given them a clean bill of health.

"Make sure you tell them we import fish from the Middle East," he barked. "Fish pedicures have been going on there for hundreds of years. Every bugger knows they're safe."

He went on to order new copies of the do's and don'ts issued to customers, making sure they were placed prominently in all treatment rooms.

"Especially the one about removing nail-varnish forty-eight hours before treatment," he ordered.

Unfortunately, *Pedi-Spa*'s damage-limitation exercise was too late for the Carlisle branch which closed immediately, pending local authority and police investigation.

An hour after her operation, Lorraine awoke disorientated from her deeply disturbed sleep.

"Where am I?" Her voice echoed in the small, over-heated room, with its white walls, white ceiling and white curtains. The glare hurt Lorraine's eyes. She felt shooting pains ricochet around her brain. "Help!" she shouted.

A young nurse dressed in a pristine white uniform strode confidently into the room.

"What is it with you people and white?" asked Lorraine.

"It's all right, dear," said the nurse, ignoring Lorraine's question. "You're in hospital. You've had an accident at the fish spa. Don't you remember?"

"I'm not sure. My head's foggy and my toe hurts."

"Don't worry, that's quite usual. It'll wear off soon and you'll be as right as rain.'

"Oh, I'm beginning to remember. Those horrible, vicious fish attacked me. I was supposed to be on a foot shoot for the spa company. They promised me five thousand pounds. Where's my mobile? I want to call my agent. I'll make sure those pigs pay for this!"

"Your belongings are in your bedside locker, but you need to rest. You're still recovering from the anaesthetic."

"Ouch!" Lorraine cried out as she felt another excruciating pain course through what was left of her right toe. "Get me gas and air," she demanded.

"You've just had a minor operation dear. We don't use gas and air. I'll get you a couple of paracetamol."

"I've got some Coke in my bag."

"I'm sorry dear. Recreational drugs are not allowed in this hospital."

"No, I mean a can of *Diet Coke*. To wash the paracetamol down."

"I'll get the paracetamol," said the nurse as she left the room.

Lorraine went through her Gucci bag: Louboutin shoes, no *Diet Coke* but her mobile still charged. She managed to get a call through to her agent.

"Ronnie? It's Lorraine."

"Lorraine babe, how are you? James told me all about the fish spa. He got some good shots of your bloody toe and the fish tank. We'll take *Pedi* to the cleaners. We might even get you a full page spread in *The Sun*. They've been after *Pedi* for years."

"I'm okay thanks, but my foot hurts like billy-o."

"Good, good. That's the thing. I'm sending Alf over to get some shots of you in hospital. Should make the dailies. Alf's good at the human interest stuff. Don't wear too much make-up. Look as ill as you can. We'll get some 'before' and 'after' pictures. It'll all help to boost interest and maybe increase compensation. Ha! Could be the best thing that's happened in your modelling career. Can I get you anything?" he asked as an afterthought.

"Just some Coke."

"Now then, we need to be careful about that."

"No, I mean *Diet Coke*. I've already had this conversation with the nurse. Get Alf to bring a can."

"Okay, sweetheart. Laters."

The registrar took his time to examine his boss's handiwork during his ward round and announced Lorraine's toe 'beautiful.' Lorraine cried. The registrar apologised for his terminology and pronounced her fit to go home.

Lorraine ordered a cab and bought copies of *The Sun* and *The Cumberland News* in the hospital kiosk. Once settled in the cab, she opened the newspapers. *The Cumberland News* led with:

Local Fish Spa Closes
Company goes into liquidation - Compensation ruled out for victims

The Sun's headline read:
FISH SWAP
Lethal Chin Chin Supplant Legal Nibblers

Sources close to the Met confirm terrorist attempt to undermine the British way of life, the freedom of independent entrepreneurs to generate income and support local economies...

There was a minute picture of Lorraine on page five, column three, and in the smallest typeface possible, the caption: 'Victim recovers in the Cumberland Infirmary'.

Her name wasn't even mentioned. Lorraine collapsed in tears.

"Are you alright lass? Can I get you anything?"

"Just Coke, please."

"Not in my cab, love!"

My Big Dog On Short Legs

*A tribute to my lovely West Highland White Terrier,
Hamish. We worked together in West Cumbria.*

He gave me anxiety and pleasure
In equal measure,
My social work assistant.
Specialising in child protection
He was an ice-breaker *par excellence.*

He loved his work riding shotgun,
Feet on the dashboard,
Savouring the blurry blue
hues of the views
speeding towards him.

He loved to walk at the end of
the day. Looking out to sea, a
twinkle in his eye. Tackle intact,
Life could only get better
With a bitch to bonk.

That's my boy!
One year and two months
deceased. Wrapped in his
crimson fleece. Ashes held
in a green silk pouch.

Placed with love on the
memorial bookshelf.
An honoured place - a
faithful friend. Hamish -
My big dog on short legs.
A love letter to my Alfa Romeo...

Carrie McIntyre

Carrie grew up in the Thames Valley and went to art school to study fashion. She began her design career in London working first in Belgravia, then in Soho – two extremes of the fashion industry.

She qualified as a lecturer in Design Studies and moved to Carlisle where she met her husband. Together they were founder members of the Stanwix Arts Theatre. She was Mistress of Robes for the 1977 Carlisle pageant, responsible for 2,000 costumes.

Carrie has worked as a costume designer and illustrator, a surface-pattern designer for ceramics and a botanical illustrator. She enjoys travel, visits to the ballet, crafts and gardening.

The Waiting Room

It was a miserable place, just a large bare room with wooden chairs arranged around the sides. A dozen girls had arrived already and were inspecting a large map of Africa pinned to one wall and Pretoria was circled in red ink. More girls arrived clutching the advertisement leaflet; most were well scrubbed and neatly dressed in cheap clothes, just as she was.

Somewhere outside a clock struck nine and a young man popped his head round the door and said "First girl, please." A big-boned girl with rosy cheeks disappeared into the next room and the rest continued to wait, stealing little sideways glances at the others. It was only when each new girl was called that Daisy felt able to have a good look. They were all young, of course; all shapes and sizes, some pretty, some not. Everyone had made an effort to look attractive although one or two had tried rather too hard and their rouged cheeks made them look like music hall dancers.

Each girl was in the other room for about ten minutes, Daisy reckoned, and just before the man called "Next, please!" she heard the slam of an outer door and the applicant was gone without ever re-entering the waiting room. After the first hour, girls began to fidget; there was foot tapping and small coughs, and two girls got up and left. Others attempted to make conversation and the young woman next to her said, "He looks nice," so she smiled but said nothing. The girl smiled back showing discoloured teeth and Daisy smelt the stale breath. The next candidate limped slightly as she made her way towards the interview room and the outer door was soon heard to slam.

By now Daisy was suspecting that any girl who had a physical defect was sent away quickly. The ones with too much make-up, the pale, tired-looking one, the painfully thin girl and the one who kept scratching at her hands; all spent very few minutes in the other room. Her neighbour was called, and sure enough she was gone for only three or four minutes before, "Next, please!" was heard again.

She had waited twenty-two years for the chance of a better life and the man in this room could end that wait. She smiled at him, a natural, happy smile that came easily to her young, healthy face as she imagined what an escape from her life of drudgery would mean. The young man had an open, intelligent face and he smiled back. "Miss?" She told him her name. "Why did you answer the advertisement, Miss Lovejoy?" "Sir, I have no family, no money and no prospects. I had little schooling but I can read and tot up – I work as a barmaid whenever I can."

"Miss Lovejoy, I have one week to buy equipment and find a wife before I sail back to South Africa. Are you willing to join me in life's adventure?" Daisy knew about South Africa from the news-sheets left in the pub. Everyone knew about the war there and of the diamond mines. She had no desire to be a miner's wife and told him so. "My dear Miss Lovejoy, I'm not going to dig!" he laughed. "I'm going to brew beer to sell to all the men who dig – that'll be my diamond mine." Daisy had no trouble envisaging the daily queues of thirsty labourers who would line up to spend what money they had on beer. "Sir, I am both willing and ready. I've waited long enough." she said holding out her hand. And so began one of South Africa's longest established breweries.

Based on a story told to the author fifty years ago by the grandson of the brewery's founder.

The Ultimate Hit

Kitty didn't want to go but Jennifer had already bought the tickets. She knew how good the actors were and Shakespeare's *The Winter's Tale* was a favourite; it was just the thought of being in the Arts Centre that made her unhappy. She chided herself for being a wimp and anyway, she thought, that philistine Dave, the manager, was unlikely to be present. She would go.

Jennifer was waiting for her and they took their seats, right in the centre of the packed auditorium. She was reminded of how tight the space was as she put her coat and bag down by her feet. The performance got underway and the temperature began to rise. Onstage anger and jealousy were brewing but in seat H13 Kitty was feeling a little uncomfortable because something seemed to be tickling her leg. She scratched through her jeans and the sensation stopped and very soon she was enjoying the play once more. By now, passion and anguish were pouring from the actors and the audience was engrossed.

Once again Kitty felt alarmed. The tickling had started again, but now it was moving slowly upwards towards her knee. A lifelong sufferer of arachnophobia she began to panic. "Oh please God, not a spider!" She realised it must be an insect that was crawling up the inside of her trouser leg and if it reached her knee it would inevitably be in contact with her skin. Perspiring, with her face burning and sweat prickling her hairline, Kitty was trapped. She was in the dark, stuck between tightly-packed theatregoers and their belongings at the most emotionally charged point of the play. She told herself, "I'll just have to sit it out because, if I stand up now, heaven knows where the thing will go and I'll never make it past all those knees and feet." To prevent the unthinkable from happening, she clamped both hands around her leg, just above the knee and waited uncomfortably for the play to end. Her tension attracted a sidelong glance from her friend. "There's a spider on me," she whispered but Jennifer wasn't interested.

Eventually, as the first act finished and the applause erupted, Kitty acted swiftly. She removed one hand from her knee, made a fist and punched her leg as hard as she could. "No spider could survive that!" she told herself, trying to ignore the fact that this thing had felt rather too hard to be spider and had been heavy enough for her to feel something drop onto her foot...

Standing up quickly, she excused herself and made straight for the ladies' toilets where she removed her shoes and trousers, and inspected the insides. There was no squashed spider, no evidence of the mini-drama she had endured. Feeling sick, she admitted to herself that it could only have been one thing to survive such a blow: a cockroach. She dressed and made her way back towards the hall.

"Kitty," called a familiar voice, "Didn't think I'd see you here." It was Mike. "What on earth's the matter?" he asked. "Are you OK?"

She told him what had happened.

"I bet that came from the space under the seating," he said. "Does the cafeteria still use that as a food store, I wonder? Anyway, tell me, why did you leave this place? It must be eight years now. I've missed seeing you."

"I had no choice," she said, smiling at the memory of their clueless younger selves, when they had been volunteers and he just a cub reporter. "It wasn't exactly professional but we did our best and it was lots of fun."

"Happy days," said Mike. "Do you remember how we used to get the last punters in? We'd dash through that storeroom, up the emergency stairs and in through the back door just in time for curtain-up."

"Yes, I remember," said Kitty. "It's a wonder we never killed ourselves climbing over all those crates and boxes in the dark, not to mention the spiral staircase. I think we were the only ones who knew it was there. Anyway, when Dave arrived to become the new centre manager he turned my role as front of house manager into a paid job. And then installed his girlfriend! All my work and loyalty over the years counted for nothing and basically I was pushed out. It took me a long time to get over the pain of that and this is the first time I've been back here. But what about you, Mike? Do you still cover these shows?"

"No, shortly after you left, the paper moved me over to the business pages which I really enjoyed. In fact I'm about to take up a new position with the *Manchester Guardian*. I told the boss I wanted to cover tonight's performance because I'd seen the company here at the start of their career and followed its progress over the years. Look, I'm really sorry you were treated so badly, Kitty, after all you did for the Centre. And the cockroach – that's quite shocking." He smiled. "I'm really pleased to see you. Don't forget to read my column, my ultimate hit," he joked. Or so she thought.

Two days later as she picked up her newspaper from the doormat, the headlines leapt off the page at her:

PUBLIC HEALTH SCARE SHUTS ARTS CENTRE

MANAGER QUESTIONED

The Shot Was...

Wayne woke up at his home in Illinois with a thumping head and a foul taste in his mouth, "Even more reason to kill the bastard!" he thought as he took a powder. He drove to the *Easimart* site and parked away from the main lot, just out of sight of the small crowd that was gathering for the much publicised Grand Opening. To be honest, 'Grand' was a bit of an exaggeration, seeing as the new *Easimart* was of very modest proportions, more of an over-sized convenience store. It was constructed on the site of a small group of run-down workshops that catered for people with old cars, electrical goods and firearms.

As the Mayor and object of his violent intent stepped up to the small dais, Wayne settled himself and took aim with his rifle through the open window. Breathe, engage, steady and squee... "aaaghhh." Right at the critical moment a bee flew straight into his ear, completely disorienting him and causing him to pull sharply on the trigger, and the gun went off. The shot was way off target, the bullet travelling in the wrong direction until it came to a large ginger cat called Melly who had been sunning himself on the garden fence. A cat of character, companion and entertainer to his owner Nev, Melly's only crime was to make his daily deposit on the manicured lawn belonging to Adrian, across the street.

Melly died instantly of course and fell back into the garden where he was discovered later by his distraught owner. Picking up his beloved pet to inspect the damage, Nev could barely believe his eyes because this cat had definitely been shot and there was only one possible culprit – that poncey Brit Adrian from across the street! Clutching the furry carcass, he hammered on Adrian's door: "Why d'ya shoot my cat, you, you *foreigner*?" Overcome, he smudged away at his tearstained face with his bloodied hand as Adrian, clearly taken aback, struggled to take in what had happened.

"I would never kill your cat, Nev. I know I complain about the crap but why can't he do it on your patch instead of mine?"

"It's Astroturf. He likes the real stuff like you've got – much softer. Anyway he's dead now and if you didn't do it, who else could've done it?"

"Well," said Adrian rather smugly, "to quote Kolakowski, 'extremely unlikely events occur every moment' and besides, I don't have a gun. Do you?"

Nev told him that he'd never had a gun. He'd always tried to keep himself out of trouble, he'd never even had a wife: "Well, y'know, they can be a bit difficult, women, never had much luck with them." Now that he was retired Nev had just wanted a quiet life with Melly. He began to sniffle again and so Adrian took him in and gave him a beer and showed him his pet bunnies in the back yard.

"Now that the new *Easimart*'s opening right here it's great because I'll be able to get cheap salad stuff for them. Past its sell-by, you know?" Adrian said by way of explanation. "Actually, I was thinking of applying for a part-time job there, they're advertising for 'mature' shelf-stackers..." Nev thought this too down-market after a life as an accountant but Adrian was still talking "...make a nice change from the stresses and strains of high finance. It'll help fill the hours and I might meet a few new folk. D'you fancy doing that, Nev? Take your mind off Melly?" Nev wasn't in the habit of stepping outside his comfort zone but what did he have to lose? Everything was changing since he'd retired early and time weighed heavily between finishing his chores and Melly coming inside for the evening.

Life rolled on quietly and uneventfully once Adrian and Nev, now buddies, started working at the food store. No stress, no worries. When he wasn't working, Nev spent time grooming his new white rabbits and fussing over his new green turf which was intended to provide luxury salads. Adrian called round to say, "Look Nev, they're showing *Watership Down* at the senior's club next week. Nev? *Neville*! It's about rabbits, Neville. Are you listening?"

"What? What did you call me? Did you call me 'Neville'? I'm not Neville." He looked quite sad for a moment and Adrian was perplexed. "What else could Nev be short for if you're not called Neville?"

Nev took a slow breath and decided to unburden himself. "My name is Cosmas – after Cosmas and Damien? The twin saints?"

"Ahh", said Adrian, "I'm Church of England. Not big on saints, I'm afraid. Apart from Saint George, of course."

Nev trusted Adrian so he continued his story: "I had a twin brother but he only lived for a few days. All I've got left of him is this," and to Adrian's astonishment Nev dropped his jeans and turned to show the back of his legs. There, down the back of one leg was a large purple splotch that looked as if it started somewhere under his boxer shorts and was making its way down the inside back of his leg. This was an unfortunate position for such a birthmark. "It was the way we were lying together in the womb, so they said. And as if it's not bad enough having that, I'm saddled with a name like Cosmas. So when people started teasing me and calling me 'Nev', because I *never* joined in with anything, I thought it sounded better than Cosmas, so I just let them think it was my real name."

Some weeks later the pair were sitting together in the *Easimart* canteen discussing the next rabbit show when they were joined by new employee Wayne. "Mind if I join you folks? We men need to stick together." It was true, the majority of employees were in fact women, some of them quite scary. If they weren't careful, the men could find themselves the objects of flirtatious advances by some of the older 'ladies'.

"So, wad'ya guys talking about?" They told him and his face broke into an ugly smirk. "Rabbits!! You guys can't be for real. Ha, rabbits! The only thing they're good for is sport." He got up and left, then returned having forgotten to pick up his lunch tray. "You woosies want to get yourselves a real hobby."

"Like what? I don't enjoy golf," said Adrian, "and I am certainly not interested in woodwork or fishing." Nev tried to think of some of the things he wasn't interested in when Wayne interrupted his thoughts "Nah, you want a man's sport, like hunting." Nev gasped. "Do you mean shooting things?"

"Well, of course you *shoot* things, otherwise there's no point in it." Wayne took his lunch and went in search of more like-minded company.

Next day Adrian had to go down to the cellar storeroom to bring up a few crates and, in the gloomy half-light, he was surprised to find Wayne emerging from the shadows in the back. As Wayne was unable to hide, he had little option but to explain his presence: "Just been looking in my ol' buddy's store," he jerked his head in the direction of the shadows. Adrian stood his ground so Wayne continued. "All the workshops that were here had cellars, so when they built this place, they kept them. This one here belonged to the motor engineers and they cleared it out properly to use. The one next door was the gunsmith's and it's still got a load of stuff in it. I was just looking to see what there was."

Adrian didn't need a searchlight to see that Wayne had pockets bulging with small, heavy objects. "You should be careful Wayne, that's stealing. I think you should tell the manager, after all, anything to do with firearms is dangerous. Especially old stuff," he added.

"I know what I'm doin'." snapped Wayne. "Just keep your nose out. I'm not doing you any harm... or your precious rabbits."

When Wayne failed to show for work the following

week, Adrian went to the manager and told him of his fears – that the grocery mart was sitting on top of a potentially lethal store of old ammunition. And, by the way, Wayne was inexplicably still absent. The manager told his uncle, the Mayor, who said they would have to shut the store whilst investigations were carried out and the place made safe, "Just think," said the Mayor, "Any one of us could have been killed in this place."

Brenda Hunter

Brenda grew up on the Raffles estate in Carlisle and often draws on the people she knew there for her stories. She has three children, two sons and a daughter, as well as several grandchildren. She is a retired SEN nurse.

Brenda enjoys writing and has been a member of the Writers' Group since it started.

Where Will We Sleep Tonight?

Jane and Zara had an invitation to go to Canada to visit their grandmother where she lived with her new husband for the last two years. The two girls were twins and lived in Yorkshire. They missed their grandmother very much. They had just finished their exams and had got excellent results. They were both starting new jobs in September. Jane was going to be a doctor, Zara a lawyer. They had eight weeks holiday and their mother said, "Grandmother is paying for you. It will be an adventure. But you are not going on your own." They looked at their mother and said together, "Oh mam, we can go on our own! We're twenty-one, so we'll be fine. You know we've been to Spain many times on our own."

"Yes, but..."

"Always a but!" "Uncle David wants to go with you. You know he's wanted to see his mother ever since his divorce."

"That's fine," said Zara and they went to pack.

Four days later they left and arrived safely at the airport in Quebec. They went through the customs with no problems, got the hire car and left with David driving.

After two hours they stopped at a big diner and had a lovely meal. After coffee they set off again, following the SatNav's directions. David didn't like the eight lanes on the freeway. The twins were glad he was with them; they couldn't have driven with so many lanes. They talked and laughed and were all in a happy mood when they reached the turn off.

"This road is better – only two lanes. It doesn't look like many use it. There's lots to see." By 4 o'clock they'd had rain and sunshine and looking around had realised what a beautiful, colourful country Canada was. After hours of driving, Zara said, "What a wind! Look at the trees. The weather changes quickly here."

"Have you noticed that not one car has passed us?" said Jane. "Look, a petrol station. We can fill the car with diesel and have a coffee." So, when that was all done they got into the car and set off again. About an hour later, the car juddered to a halt, so David got out to check. It was now 8pm and they could see buildings in the distance. The girls got out to join David and gave him his coat. They put their own on too, as they were very cold. David said that the engine had ceased up. "We will all have to walk to the buildings ahead because I am not leaving you in the car on your own." So with coats, light bags and a few other things they set off.

The wind was so strong and David held their hands. They could see the lights of a town ahead and they kept on the road so they wouldn't get lost. They hadn't gone far when heard a noise that frightened them. They turned to hug each other and inexplicably felt they were falling. Shaken, they suddenly found themselves on the ground, lying on a pile of leaves. The girls started to cry. David fumbled in his pocket and found his torch. They seemed now to be in a forest. They could no longer see the town ahead, and had lost sight of the road too. They heard horses galloping, then a cry from the bushes: "Stay together. Come, hide in this bush. Be quiet." About eighteen Indians went by with war paint on.

"Mohawk," David thought remembering his history from school. "Either this is a film set or we've gone back in time! Stay together, girls." They moved slowly and soon stumbled on the bodies of a man, a woman and a small boy in a burned out carriage. "It's not a film set. We have slipped through time!"

The twins looked so scared. "You can't mean that, Uncle David. We were on a road. We didn't really fall, did we? But the town's no longer there - and where has the road gone?"

"And actors don't really die on film sets, do they?" He hugged them both and said, "We should sleep soon and see what tomorrow brings."

Zara looked troubled. "But where will we sleep tonight?" she asked.

Childhood Memories

One of my childhood memories was potato picking. My brothers and I would get up early and although I can't remember three of us on a bicycle, only last week my brother, Gerald, told me we went to the farm that way. We stood in the farmyard, waiting for the man to come. He pointed to us and either said 'you and you', or 'you - go home'. Then we were put on a trailer and taken to the field. We each were told where to stand and had a furrow to work.

It was back-breaking work. I only went three times; the following year I remember pulling a face when I recalled the backache I'd had. I was happy to stay home and do without the money! Gerald and Cyril were up and away for many years. It changed a lot over that time; they eventually had a conveyor belt that they'd take the potatoes off to be bagged. Gerald went much more than either of us. He became friends with the farmer's son, David Jenkins, and was soon eating with the family in the house. I remember Gerald being sad when we found out David had died young of an illness.

Most of us from Raffles Council estate went at one time or another. It was fun all being together. Cyril, my eldest brother, never liked going but liked very much the seven and six a day that we made! His friend, Tony, never went - his mother gave him eight shillings not to go! She did not want him working so young. Alan's brothers were working and gave him pocket money so he didn't go either. We got the week off school to go. I think it was August and it was always sunny. I remember I bought a pair of blue cotton jeans in the Woolworth's store for three and six with the money I made.

At a certain time, when we were bent-backed picking potatoes, the farmer's wife came with a tea urn and some rock buns. We stopped working and enjoyed the rest. I remember it was hard after that rest to start again.

The summers we had when we were still at school always seemed hot. We went to Raffles children's park to play and paddle in the pool, or sometimes a few mothers took us to the river Eden with jam sandwiches and a bottle of water and we played all day. I learned to swim in the river. I remember a part we children called 'the bubbly'. It was next to the electricity power station. We liked it there as it was warm and no-one ever said we were not to go in the water. We never knew if it was dangerous or not, but over the years none of us came to any harm. Our mothers sat on the bank and talked while we laughed and swam. Then we walked home, happy. Sometimes we got a bag of chips and we ate them on the way home. I think they were threepence, paid for with the three-penny bits we had then. We asked for scrapings - bits of batter - and got those free.

We were allowed to play around the street-lamp outside our house till nine o'clock at night, then our mothers would shout for us to come in for bed. We had games of marbles or spinning top and skipping, even jumping on the privet hedge and knocking on doors and running away. Oh happy days! Where have they gone? Oh, yes - we grew up!

The Awakening

In the year 2030, the atom bomb had caused devastation to the world. Rebels were intent on destroying all humans, even themselves. Scientists all over the world had saved thousands of people and had frozen many of them. Today was the day some were to be woken.

Zoe was coming to when she heard a nurse say, "How long will it take her to wake up?'

"You obviously haven't been here long if you have to ask me, nurse Dana," said Counsellor Tancred. "It is different for each person. I will be with her until she adjusts to her new life."

Doctor Hall said, "Look she is coming round now. Hello, dear. I have been looking after you for the last 23 years." Zoe tried to sit up but needed the nurse to help her. After a short time she remembered being put to sleep

"How long have I been asleep," she asked

"For 150 years," said Tancred. "How do you feel?"

"I feel all right, but tired." ·

"Come and see if you can walk." Once out of the chamber Zoe walked very well.

"Can I go outside and have some air?" she said. "Oh, I have lots of questions!"

The Doctor and Tancred did not put on infiltration masks but Zoe was told to wear one. Once it was on, the doctor fixed a bracelet to Zara's wrist. He said, "This is your identification bracelet, which you must never take off. We all have them. Later, you won't need a mask, once you've got used to the air." Then Tancred explained he would stay with her for a while and answer all her questions.

She looked at the white, skin-tight suits they were all wearing. "Are these the clothes everyone wears?"

"We all wear the same," said the nurse. Zoe smiled, then Tancred said, "Door open!" which it did without a switch or button being pressed. Zoe noticed but said nothing. As she walked outside and noticed the blue sky, she felt a tear trickle down her cheek. Her emotions were stirred. She felt that something wasn't right but knew it was a rare and unusual world. She was glad to be alive. They walked across a paved square where people passed by talking, but no one looked happy. Not one smile did Zoe see. There was a very high wall but beyond the wall Zoe saw hills, scorched brown by the sun. The buildings were not brick built looked like metal with a lot of precise welding.

As they walked, Zoe said, "Can I speak to someone who was frozen at the same time as me?"

"We are taking you to see your sister and your Uncle Frank," said Tancred.

As they went into a large room, Zoe fell into the arms of her sister and uncle. They hugged each other and wept, each glad to be alive. "Do we still have mobile phones?" asked Zoe.

"No," said Tancred. "When a baby is born we insert a chip inside it and when they are seven we activate it. We can communicate without holding a device."

"Do people still have asthma and other ailments?"

"No, we can sort out most health problems,"

Zoe then said, "I can't wait to go and explore."

"No, you can't do that," said Tancred, with irritation in his voice.

Zoe remembered a film she had seen in her other life called *Logan's Run* where people lived in a dome and died at the age of 30. They could not get away. She felt that she was in a similar situation. They sat talking for a long time.

Zoe saw a lovely fountain in the corner. "Can I get a drink from the fountain, please?"

"No," said Tancred and he touched his wrist and asked for refreshments to be brought. A girl dressed the same as everyone else brought in an electric trolley full of food and drink. Zoe thought how sad she looked. She enjoyed the food and her drink; she only wanted water but this was okay.

*   *   *   *   *

Zoe awoke in a room in a round bed and wondered how she had got there. She could remember drinking and enjoying the food but not going to bed. Then she worried about the wristband they had given her and hoped it was not making her a prisoner. Her freedom would not be easy to gain, so she decided she would listen for a few days to find out what was going on and why people looked so sad. Materialism was not visible at all, that was good. Everyone was equal that was progress. All could drive a car on the automated highway. People said where they wanted to go and the car took them, but there were still limits as to how far they went. There was always a counsellor close by. Zoe had learned a lot on her first day, but she knew she would want to leave and live free. What would the next day bring, and how could she drink and stay awake? This life was a great new adventure!

Barbara Robinson

Barbara was born in Threlkeld near Keswick, where she went to secondary school. She became a nurse in Carlisle. She is married, has three children and six grandchildren.

Barbara is a long-time member of Carlisle Writers' Group.

Winter

Oh how I hate the winter!
The endless hours of darkness,
The frost, the fog, the rain.
A deep depression plagues me
Till spring comes round again.

The grey skies match my feelings,
The coldness fills my bones.
Not for me the snow scene,
It produces moans and groans!

I suppose it can be beautiful
When skies are blue and gold,
But even then what comes to mind
It's still just far too cold.

Confidence

Right or wrong, this won't take long,
I don't know where to start,
It's such a massive subject
I'll only take a part.

Some people think they're always right,
They get right up your nose.
They won't admit they're ever wrong,
Such confidence it shows!

Some people are so insecure,
They think they're always wrong.
They need some gentle coaxing
To help them get along.

But most of us are in between
And we all have our strengths
And have our own opinions,
And stress them at great lengths.

And who's to say who's right or wrong?
We'll all be judged in time.
And now I'm going to finish this,
Because I've just run out of rhyme.

Four Days In The Kruger Park

After many invitations from relatives to visit them in South Africa, we finally made the trip in 1988. The highlight of the holiday was a four-day excursion to the Kruger, the internationally famous game reserve in the Transvaal. The reserve is a huge slice of acacia and mopane tree-covered veld covering an area the size of Wales, surrounded by a perimeter fence. It was first opened to the public in 1926.

We drove from cousin David's farm in the Drakensberg Mountains in a most-welcome air-conditioned car, stopping on the way to buy mangoes and papayas from a roadside stall.

The reserve has several gates, and we entered by one called Numbihek, and made our way in a leisurely manner to our first camp. The weather was perfect; the rains had been plentiful, and everywhere was lush and green. Baby animals were very much in evidence, especially impala. They seemed to have no fear of motor vehicles, and we were able to see them at close-quarters. Thanks to David's sharp eyes, and knowledge of what was what, we could spot other, more shy antelopes among the bushes, beautiful creatures such as kudu, bushbuck, waterbuck, and steenbuck. Not so beautiful creatures were also plentiful, like quarrelsome baboons and warthog. The larger trees had vervet monkeys peering out of the foliage. We were entranced by the sheer abundance of wild life.

For the first two nights we were staying at a camp called Ekukuza, which consisted of a series of small thatched huts containing camp beds and a shower, which were perfectly adequate for our needs. We had dinner in the camp restaurant. Buffalo was on the menu, and mealie porage. Just outside the restaurant was a small fenced-off pond; a bit of old log floating on the water turned out to be a crocodile. The camp gates were closed at six prompt, and if you were not in by then, it was hard luck! We went to bed early hoping to make a five-thirty start next morning.

After a quick cup of coffee, we set off for a full day's game spotting. The ground was rather less well covered with scrub than the day before, and almost immediately we came upon zebra, giraffes, wildebeest and an enormous tortoise.

We were ravenous, and stopped for breakfast at a picnic spot; we had bacon, eggs and chops cooked on a portable barbeque, or brie as the South Africans call them. The toilet facilities were about a hundred yards out in the bush, with neither a roof nor a door; I wondered vaguely what would happen if a lion decided to wander in while I was in there!

We carried on driving around, choosing the dirt tracks rather than the cement roads, as there was more chance of seeing a greater diversity of animals. We saw hippos in a nearby waterhole, and several other varieties of antelope, duikers, hartebeest, and a very small one perched on a rock looking for all the world like a *Babycham* advert, called a klipspringer. Then on the other side of the stream we saw our first elephants having a wash. We never knew what would be around the next corner. We followed a secretary bird striding solemnly down the road, reminding me of childhood Rupert books. It was a birdwatcher's paradise. We saw storks, ostriches, hornbills, egrets, ibises, kingfishers and, of course, vultures and the ghastly maribou storks. Circling overhead were eagles and buzzards. Tired but exhilarated, we went back to camp and had another barbeque.

The next day we went further into the park to a camp called Satara. On the way we passed a pack of wild dogs which made David very excited as apparently they were quite rare. I didn't warm to them myself as they looked like jackals and hyenas, which we also saw.

We were feeling slightly disappointed that we had not seen any lions when suddenly we turned a corner, and lying at the side of the track were three lionesses. Unhurriedly, they got up and went round behind some tall grasses, where we could see them watching us.

A little further on, we came upon a group of elephants, just crossing the road. A huge old matriarch decided that we were too close so, after shepherding the babies across the road, she turned, flapped her ears, stamped her foot and set off towards us. By this time I was frozen to the spot and my husband was half way out of the car in a panic, but David was imperturbably changing the film in his camera, and Aunt Isobel was sitting in the back as unflappable as ever! Mercifully it was only a warning; shortly after we returned to England, we read about a tourist being killed by a charging elephant in the Kruger Park.

The following day, we set off on the long journey back out of the Park, stopping at picnic spots with wonderful names like Mzanzene, Nhalanguleni and Tshokwana, each equipped with large chest freezers full of iced drinks, out in the open air, and park rangers standing around with rifles at the ready. We saw a most amusing sight at a man-made waterhole; a troop of baboons was running along the edge and diving in like children at a swimming pool while a senior baboon kept watch from an old tree stump.

We spent our last night at the Park at a camp called Berg En Dal. It was an idyllic spot and I made a mental note to go back there some day. It had been a marvellous four days

- no newspapers, no television, no telephones, just the great outdoors, African style.

Anne Carter

Anne was born in Cockermouth and educated in Cumbria, France and the United States. She has married twice; her first husband was an American, and they have one son who lives in Los Angeles. She has two grandchildren.

Anne has worked in the theatre in the UK and California; she studied Russian ballet in Britain and France, and drama in Britain and New York. She studied sculpting, languages and sports science; she also worked in law in this country. Locally, she directed the Mary Queen of Scots section of the 1977 pageant at Carlisle Castle.

On The Border

"I have asked if they will include squid on the menu," I heard him say.

"I have never eaten squid. I don't suppose I ever will," I said.

He looked a bit scathing.

"I like it," he said. "I ordered some red wine."

"I don't drink wine," I said.

We were in Ensenada. I like Baja, as long as I can go south of Tijuana. A border town never knows to which side it belongs.

I decided to leave him to it and said I was going for a walk. I loved the beaches, they had not at that time been ruined. People had not invaded them, and one could still see the sea anemones.

"Squid," I thought. "Squid, squid, squid." Soon there would be no squid. The world would have eaten them all.

I began to run through the waves. It was very calm that

night, the sun was setting and I doubt if one could ever find such glorious sunsets as there are along the western coast of Baja. The orange was dazzling like a fire opal. There was still a streak of blue, and as the sea blended with the sky, it looked like a giant lampshade was hanging over everything. I passed a fisherman.

"Como le va?"

"Bien, gracias."

He was right. He had already had a small catch. I wondered if I would ever come back this way again, once I had left the continent. Would I ever see Mexico again? I had always loved it. I sat down and surveyed the darkening sky. A few stars began to twinkle. I thought how near it was to Hollywood, where a different type of star resided. I wondered what would have happened if there had not been a gold rush.

I had been born in a quiet, isolated community, which did not suit me at all. And yet this was too quiet and isolated but it had the glorious sun and the warmth of a summer night. Suddenly I knew how Aldous Huxley had written his Music at Night. He too was British but loved the very pleasures that I loved here.

I spotted a cruise ship coasting along the horizon. There were a lot of lights sparkling, and looking at my watch, I pictured couples dancing after having dined. I wondered where they were going. I had never liked the idea of cruising - lots of people on the one moving object, floating on the ocean. The claustrophobia of not being to get off terrified me. I would not be able to run away and hide.

I thought about the squid again. I imagined he would have drunk so much red wine that he would be unapproachable. Anyway, I did not want to approach him. I did not want to go back.

I walked into a little seaside village and could smell burnt tortillas. Someone must be eating chilli con carne and enchiladas. I had not eaten, so I decided to try and get a salad. I found a little restaurant with a balcony overlooking the sea. I was not going back. I had, at least, come to a decision. "Adios, mi amigo!"

The Brown Bag

Marcus was standing on a platform at Knightsbridge Station. The train was late as usual. Marcus was singing under his breath, "Brexit, Brexit, Brexit." He was carrying his football in a brown paper bag. He thought he knew every nook and cranny of this station because the trains were always late. Anyway, he set off again and put his parcel on one of the chairs. He gave himself three minutes, and after two and a half he heard the train and dashed onto the platform. The doors opened and he disappeared inside. He was still humming "Brexit."

He got off at the next station and started to walk home, when he suddenly remembered the football. He had just enough money to go back and take a short cut that he knew well to retrieve the brown bag. He noticed the bag had been moved onto the platform. He grabbed it and was fortunate enough to catch a train immediately. He wondered if he had got the right platform but reassured himself as he had found the bag. He had only just been allowed to use the Tube by himself, this being his ninth birthday, and only between Knightsbridge and South Kensington.

He went directly to Dominique's house, Dominique also being nine years old. They both went to Marcus's house to watch a video of *Giant Tank 2*. When the movie was over, Marcus remarked, "I wonder if we use those tanks in the Yemen?"

"I don't know," said Dom. "Are we at war with Yemen?"

"Oh, yes," said Marcus importantly. "It's very useful to have a father in the Secret Service, particularly as I have a hidey-hole in the drawing room to which I go when Papa entertains his influential friends.

Dom though how lucky Marcus was. *His* father was only an Honourable, whatever that was. Marcus went on, "That's why I know we are at war with Yemen and Germany," he said importantly.

"How do you know that?" asked Dom.

"Because of Brexit!"

"What does that mean?" said Dom.

"I don't know, except that it means we are at war. We were going to France for our holidays but we can't go now because of the war."

"Do you think we will be able to fight?" said Dom.

"Oh, I imagine so. It might delay our CE to Eton," said Marcus.

Meanwhile the police and the Foreign Office were in a total panic. The Brown Bag had disappeared. They had cleared the station. The demolition squad were there, but no Brown Bag. On the adjoining platform, they had found *a* brown bag, and had followed normal procedure, only to find that they were about to blow up a football.

Dom and Marcus were continuing their conversation.

"Where is Yemen?" asked Dom.

"I don't know. I think it's in Central America."

"It must be difficult fighting in Europe *and* America," continued Dom.

"Yes," said Marcus. "Our army has been dee-plee-ted,"

"What does that mean?"

"I don't know, but it must be much bigger if we can fight on two fronts. Let's go and play football."

They went to pick up the brown bag.

"This is not the football. I must have gone to the wrong platform," said Marcus.

"What is it?" asked Dom.

"It looks like somebody's parcel. I don't think I'll open it. You can't be too careful these days, Mama says. I'll put it in the waste bin just to make sure that it's safe."

The waste bin had been put in the lane with all the others for collection, so Marcus wasn't particular about which one he put it in.

"No football," he said, "so shall we watch *Giant Tank 3?*"

"No, let's go and play in the woods behind the house," said Dom.

They were both climbing a very large fir tree when there was an explosion.

"Gosh, the war is coming very close," said Marcus.

"Yes," said Dom. "We may be called up sooner than we think."

When it was time for tea, they went in the back door, just in time to see Marcus's father disappearing with the police. He stopped and told the boys that Marcus's mother was at the hairdressers, and that the explosion had been in the lane next to the house. The police and Secret Service needed him urgently to investigate the explosion. Fortunately, no one had been hurt.

"Might as well have tea in the kitchen," he told the boys. "It is chocolate and chocolate ice-cream for a special treat."

Cheap Red Wine And Garlic Butter

Alain Raquin was lying on a sunbed by a pool at his father's chateau. His father was in Paris, his mother had said that Papa was "propping up the Government." Alain privately thought that his father was not propping up anything but that he would be waking up with his mistress. Alain knew the gossip, his mother chose to ignore it. Alain ruminated on whether he would choose the same route. His father had been a great friend of Francois Mitterand, and he, Alain, had very much liked the man. Nicholas Sarkozy had had other women before Carla. What would his *own* future be?

He knew that to have a wife and mistress was normal for the French. Divorce was expensive and confession made it easy to reconcile the two. Father Trondeau was regularly at their house and was a very tolerant man and Alain felt sure it was not too difficult to say a few "Hail Marys." He knew that his father had made his mother a very wealthy woman and it was a matter of honour and chivalry to makes one's mistress equally secure. France demanded it. He knew that many women, once reputation was established and families completed, were not particularly interested in having sex with their husbands. It was common sense. He did not know if his mother had a lover but he imagined it was quite possible. It was, after all, normal.

Alain's own girlfriend was Sophie, the daughter of the Contessa Taglioni, a very pretty girl, who had a large dowry. His parents, together with her parents, totally approved. They were anxious that the young couple should become engaged and not wait too long to get married. The sooner the breeding started, the better. Alain felt he had a few more wild oats to sow before he settled down but had not yet had a mistress as such, which he felt was a useful necessity. He considered that too many children would not be a good idea and decided that two would be quite enough.

Alain was attending the Faculty de Medecine in the Quartier Latin. He had only one more year to go. His family home was in Eliqluen, home to the Casino de Paris, a beautiful suburb. Alain had friends of different nationalities, and knew that there were different attitudes in different countries. Moreover, he had travelled a lot and noted similarities and differences.

He decided to go into Paris. It was August and most Parisians had left the capital. He showered and called Manuel to bring his Porsche to the front of the house. After going to see his mother, and tell her he would skip dinner tonight, he drove off to his friend Claude's house in St Germain de Pres. He stopped off to buy a bottle of Veuve Clicot, and to let Claude know he was coming. Claude was also a student of medicine. His family was in Tunis and he was Jewish. He was in his final year and saw it as imperative to return to his own country which was presently in some turmoil. The country needed doctors. Claude had a girlfriend back home, with whom he had a child. He would always return to her, but he had many relationships in Paris.

They decided to go to an expensive night club in the Elysees. They dined well and had more good champagne. Alain was spending the night at Claude's flat. As they were about to leave, an announcement came over the tannoy system, and the owner of the restaurant came out to tell them that the Café Marseilles had been blown up. There were many casualties and doctors needed. He gave out the address and Alain and Claude took a taxi to that arrondisement.

It was chaos and difficult to get through the chaos to the wounded. *They* of course were permitted and needed. After Alain had spent hours helping, he looked up and his mind was in a spin. Is this the way the other half lives? He was overwhelmed by the smell of cheap red wine, garlic butter, and surrounded by blood and corpses.

Alison Nixon

Alison lives in the Borders village of Newcastleton. She has worked in Carlisle for Enesco, a firm making ceramic figurines, for almost thirty years.

Although she finds it hard always to find the time, Alison enjoys writing and, moving away from submitting work to agents, is venturing into self-publishing. She was encouraged to join CWG after a chance meeting with another group member at a creative writing course; she enjoys being in the group.

Alison is a keen member of a walking group based in her village; she likes to relax watching rom-coms or crime thrillers.

The Brown Leather Bag

I see you out of the corner of my eye, watching me. I admit defeat, dropping my bag at my feet, and turn to face you. You do not speak. But then again, why should you? After all, I dumped you. I put out my hand and run it over your body, but you're cold and stiff. I can still vaguely smell that familiar scent on you. Daisy. Suddenly, I'm beside myself, and take you in my arms and hug you.

Before I know it, we're heading for the till and you're slipping between the sheaves of plastic and I carry you, carry you from your 'prison'. I knew I'd made a mistake when I had that clear-out, and put my favourite brown leather bag in the second hand shop.

Now wiser, and £2.00 lighter, we head for home where you belong.

Crimson Freedom

The shot was crimson in colour, I noticed; a syphon of blood, almost, in a thick glass tumbler. Nevertheless, I threw my head back and gagged as the burning liquid took the skin of my throat. I slammed the tumbler down on the table and was given slightly hysterical applause from the assembled company. I tried not to gag and I swear my eyes became crossed.

"Well, who's for another?" I cried, and out of nowhere, as if by magic, another little tumbler appeared. Crimson-green, or maybe blended-frog green? It was getting hard to tell, or care. I'd finally lost my virginity - well, my liqueur virginity. You see, I'm a changed woman these days. Gone is the six-gins-a-year-girl; my birthday and new year. I was a settled suburban housewife of fifty plus, bogged down in the daily grind of the school run, part-time job in the local bakery, husband on nine-to-five, a cup of tea on a Saturday night to 'wet my whistle' before the 'typhoon' of married ways. That was as exciting as it got. Call me old-fashioned, married before my time, maybe, and to a much older man. Maybe I became 'old' before my time.

Now? Now, I've ripped off the covers and it's a brand new me! Ta-da!

This all came about after I surprised my husband with a piece of birthday cake at his office one night. He was working late, again; he worked so hard - or so I thought. I did find him working hard, working hard on top of his secretary, the ever-efficient Miss Scott, on his office desk, no less. He'd skewered to the woodwork, so to speak, like some wanton beast you see fighting for its life on the National Geographic Channel, eyes bulging, tongue hanging out. She had that fresh, crisp rosy glow, like a frog being mounted by an alligator!

Well, he certainly got his cake and ate it that night when I pushed it into his face! Really, such a waste of a classic vanilla sponge! He moved out, to his mum's. The children go to see him every Saturday morning and Wednesday nights. They are good kids.

Me? I joined Slimming World, got a new wardrobe and a full-time job in the local chemist, a makeover and two toy boys. Well, that's all I'll admit to. And now we have a dog! I don't even like dogs.

So now, here we are at Blackpool for my sister's hen party. It's a rare, glorious evening as we teeter from bar to bar, kisses from strangers, trying to keep upright in these heels… The night is a blur.

Back at the B'n'B, I fight my way out of my clothes and fall on the bed. I'm sharing the room with Suzanne and Bethany, who, remarkably, are asleep already and snoring from one end or the other. I can't sleep and my stomach starts to churn. I make it to the toilet bowl just in time. I notice the shot of liquid is crimson, with a hint of green. I think I may die tomorrow.

I Knew It Was You

I knew it was you as I watched through the crack in my bedroom curtains. I'd been sitting waiting for a whole hour, but I'd have keenly sat for a week of hours. I didn't need to hear the sound from your lips, feel your breath on my cheek and your scent in my nostrils. I just knew it was my Fred.

As I watched you turn the corner into our road, my heart leaped as your shadow danced along the pavement through the cold frosty night, past the cars and vans. My boy was coming home. I felt almost faint with relief. Though I won't lie, I feared I'd never see you again. You had been gone two long days and nights, making me fret with worry. Usually, you just storm out, off down the garden, when we don't see eye to eye, which seems to be more frequent as you get older. You always had an eye for the ladies. We didn't part on good terms.

When I came home and caught you with that bird in your clutches, it was the last straw. The house was a mess, I'd had a bad day and I did say things I regret. When I lobbed Aunty Winnie's nasty cheap vase at you, smacking you on the head and drenching you like a drowned cat, I truly believed I'd gone too far and you left me.

I waited until you were walking up our path before I dared leave my warm, cosy chair by the window. I was scared in case I made a movement or sound to startle and scare you off, even though you were outside and I was in the house. I listened as I heard the door click downstairs and I knew you were inside. I breathed such a sigh of relief, I can tell you, and I raced down the stairs two at a time to welcome my man home.

There you were, already sitting on your favourite chair

in the living room, awaiting your supper and as always staring in awe at rubbish on the telly. Soaps always seem to grab your attention. Though we're mad soap junkies in our house, watching a good nature programme together can have us both enthralled and relaxed, especially on those black winter nights. I call your name and you look at me with such love I could burst. You follow me into the kitchen in silence and as usual take my seat, making yourself comfy. I begin to tell you about my day, our little spat of forty-eight hours earlier all forgotten. I take your favourite meal from the fridge, tuna. Well, I knew you'd return sooner rather than later. I had to stay positive, you see; positive thinking, you know, works wonders, as they always told me at the W.I. I set your dinner out and once you're finished, I take you in my arms for a longed-for cuddle, running my hands through your short ginger hair, feeling your breath and whiskers on my cheek, the faint smell of hay tingling my nose.

To some people you're just a cat, but to me, you're my confidante and companion. As I enter my ninetieth year, Fred, you're my best friend.

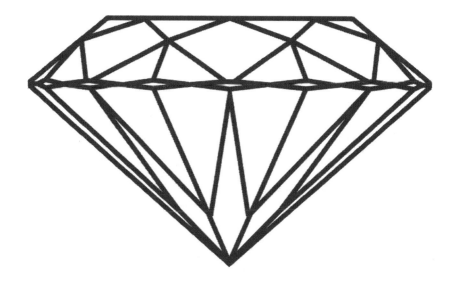

Alfa Bennett

Alfa has been creating stories and poetry since her school days, when she was encouraged by inspirational teachers. Working with children and writing stories for her own family ensured she kept on writing over the years.

Alfa joined Carlisle Writers in 2000; the invaluable support and encouragement of other group members has helped her move forward with her writing.

Diamonds In The Dust

Fred Jones had been a small time burglar all his adult life, following in his father's footsteps and keeping up the family tradition.

Reaching the age of fifty, he decided it was time to go for the big one. Until then he had been like a cat with nine lives; the police were well aware of his activities, but were unable to pin the crimes on him because of a lack of evidence and watertight alibis. His wife had always been supportive of his illicit activities but she had begun to pressure him to retire.

So Fred enlisted the aid of his partner in crime, Henry Smith, and they planned a heist on the Hatton Garden Jewellers, where the vaults were filled to capacity with diamonds. After careful surveillance and meticulous planning, all went according to plan. On the evening of the heist the two pals left the building with bags laden with diamonds.

Then Fred's luck finally ran out. Looking up at a set of traffic lights, he spotted a security camera nestling on the top - a new addition! It hadn't been there the day before. Too late to do anything about it, he knew that this time he would be rumbled. He needed damage limitation. Splitting up from Henry, his partner in crime, he raced home with his share of the spoils.

Maggie heard the door open, but as was her way stayed in bed, glad only that he was back. She could hear thumps and thuds downstairs which seemed to go on forever. Then finally he came to bed.

"We'll be getting a visit from the cops in the morning," he said. I got caught on a bloody camera." Maggie's heart sank. So at last Fred had run out of lives. "Let's get some sleep, love."

As Fred predicted, the police were banging on the door at ten o'clock the next morning. Fred and Maggie were getting on with routine jobs; Maggie was hoovering and Fred washing the kitchen floor. An intensive search of every inch of the house for diamonds brought no results. There was not a diamond in sight. Standing watching the search, Fred whispered to Maggie, "Don't worry love, Henry's got the diamonds."

In spite of the police not finding any spoils, Fred was arrested, charged and remanded in custody. Three months later he was found guilty and sentenced to five years. Luckily, Henry had avoided the camera and fled abroad.

In the months following Fred's incarceration, Maggie was devastated and couldn't find any energy to do anything around the house. She just sat and stared out of the window as if watching for Fred to return. But Maggie was tough, so she gave herself a good talking to and took the vacuum cleaner out of the cupboard; it had always been her favourite household job. Fred used to tease her about it. "You love it more than you love me, Maggie."

She whizzed round the downstairs and then went up to the bedroom. Vacuuming around, the cleaner suddenly sucked up a stray sock of Fred's, and ground to a halt. Maggie opened it up, took out the cardboard bag and shook its contents out onto a newspaper. The bag was full and dust went everywhere. Poking around in the dirt for the sock, she spotted some small shiny beads. Picking one up, she gasped. Maggie had discovered diamonds in the dust, and lots of them. Clever Fred had hoovered them up the night of the heist!

When Fred had said, "Henry's got the diamonds," he hadn't meant Henry Smith, his accomplice. He'd meant Henry the Hoover!

"Wow," said Maggie, "You clever old sod!"

Illicit Liaisons

In the hotel bedroom, as she was getting ready to go out for the evening, Maggie was feeling apprehensive, nervous and excited. A pile of discarded dresses, trousers and tops littered the large king-size bed and the pale green carpet was dotted with scattered shoes of every style and hue. Finally deciding on a moss-green silk dress and gold stilettos, she was, after a twirl in the long mirror, ready – ready to go. Grabbing a coat, Maggie went down to the foyer to get her taxi.

There was a soft drizzle falling as she arrived at the popular Tequila restaurant; the place where she had first met her husband all those years ago, the same restaurant she was now entering alone. As she stepped out of the swing doors, the head waiter greeted her and took her coat. She looked around and stepped back in time.

Nothing had changed! The faint odour of burning

tortillas hung in the air, invading the room; the red lampshades were casting a rosy light onto each of the heavy, bare wooden tables. The click-clack of the waiters' black polished shoes on the floor mingled with the clatter of plates from the kitchen beyond, as the doors swung open and shut.

On reaching the table she had booked, Maggie ordered a Pinot Noir, and asked the hovering waiter to give her a few minutes. She reached for the large embossed menu, hoping that the prices inside were not representative of the menu's size. When the food arrived, it was delicious, the squid cooked and served just as she liked it.

Maggie began to relax and look around at her fellow diners. Every table was occupied and then, there he was! Sitting alone at a corner table on the opposite side of the room. Good looking, though balding! Great body too, she observed, in a dark suit beneath which he wore a black trendy T-shirt, not the conventional white polyester shirt and stodgy tie that most of the other male diners were wearing.

She couldn't take her eyes away from him. Maggie felt red hot. She fancied him rotten. "Stop it, Maggie!" she told herself. "This isn't you," but when he looked across, their eyes locked. She waved and he responded with a charming smile. This couldn't be happening. But it was...

He got up and walked across to her and held out his hand. "I'm Joe," he said. "May I join you?"

Maggie noticed he had a firm grip.

The waiter arrived as Joe sat down and ordered a bottle of Pinot Noir! They made small talk, discussing everything from the weather to politics, and their dreams for the future, as if they had known each other for years. The time flew past. They finished the bottle of wine between them.

Maggie drank most of it.

Near to ten o'clock, he looked around the emptying restaurant, fixed her with his smouldering eyes and said, "How about we go outside?"

Maggie thought to herself, "Okay, this is it. You can leave or you can go out there with him!"

He paid both their bills and once outside they walked side by side along the nearly deserted streets. She was aware of his presence, the nearness of a strong man. It was thrilling, comforting and reassuring at the same time. The light drizzle of the early evening had stopped and the wet pavements shone silver in the glow of the street lights.

Entering her hotel, there was no need for words as they headed for the lift. Once inside, he lightly touched and kissed her hair and slipped a muscly arm around her shoulders. Outside her room, he took the key-card from her and opened the door.

Inside they stood motionless and stared at each other. Then, taking her hand, Joe said, "The chemistry is still there, Maggie, isn't it? Even after twenty years of marriage."

"Yes, Joe. It's been a wonderful anniversary."

But Joe had the last loving words. Throwing his hands up and laughing as he looked around, he said, "My God, Maggie, after twenty years together I still haven't got you to hang up your clothes. What a tip! Oh well, there's always next year! Come on woman; if we're to use this bed tonight, let's get moving!!"

Midnight Deadline

It's about time I ended it. The deadline is midnight! If he hasn't walked through that door by then, then that's it. That clinches it.

I've been thinking about it for ages, agonising over it, ever since I began to suspect that there was someone else in his life. It's the little things that give it away; the musky perfumed smell on his scarf, the tinge of pink on his hankies, the mobile phone rammed back in his pocket whenever I appear. Then there's the extra miles on the clock and the cache of six pairs of underpants; Ted Baker boxer shorts, still in packets and hidden under his usual white-turned-grey Y-fronts. And all those meetings after work. The hours he works, we should be bloody millionaires by now! Then he returns home late and immediately refuses the supper I've lovingly prepared. He'd eaten out, he said. I bet he had! I can't bear it any longer. I want out. I don't want my life any more. I want to end it now. Well, not quite now. Midnight is my deadline.

The lady on the Samaritan's phone line, bless her, so calm and supportive, just let me talk, but what did she know? I told her my life was crap and I wanted to end it all, and - hear this - she asked me if I was suicidal. Well I ask you! I put the phone down.

Everyone has their own reasons for being alive and staying alive, and, conversely, their reasons for wanting out of the life they have, to die.

I've made all the arrangements. My bills are all paid up to date. I've written letters to my friends, put money in my children's bank accounts and left them personal letters, which will explain why I don't want to be here... but no note for him.

My eyes stray to the clock on the wall, which has hung there for twenty-five years, a hideous wedding present from his mother. God, I hate that clock! Didn't like her either, always putting me down! Eleven o'clock and I can hear on the television in next room, the New Year celebrations from Trafalgar Square.

I've made a logical decision. I've picked the bones of it bare. When I look at reports of suicide in the newspapers, it usually says in the coroner's report, "While of unsound mind." I think that's rubbish! If life is unbearable and bad things after bad keep happening, then a sound rational mind would change it and end it. A good, happy and successful life, though, would only be ended by an unsound mind. Well, that's what I believe.

This life of mine is a mockery, unbearable, so after careful, sober contemplation I've made my decision. It's about time I put an end to it. Time is ticking and running out: he isn't back yet. The midnight deadline is almost upon me and I know - there, I've said it at last - he won't be back tonight. But I will wait, while this life ticks away, held by a fragile thread of hope.

I hear strains of Auld Lang Syne on the TV. Time to go! With a last look around the room, I leave and go upstairs to make my final preparations.

I'm smiling, my road ahead is clear.

The airport is heaving like a giant anthill as I arrive, just as the clock strikes one. "Happy New Year, luv," the taxi driver shouts after me. I look up and see my flight details, which will end this miserable existence and take me to the start of a new life in Spain.

I spare a moment's thought for the caring Samaritan lady. Sorry pet, for me you got it wrong. Suicidal? That wasn't the road for me. Not bloody likely. Sod him… I'm off to Spain.

Other books by members of Carlisle Writers' Group
available from Amazon...

Two of Carlisle Writers' Group's previous anthologies:
Write Again! and *Write On!*

John Nevinson:
Nothing Can Possibly Go Wrong! and *A Sting In The Tale*

Roberta Twentyman:
Tales From Hatcher's Hollow and *In Another Life*

 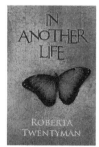

Susan Cartwright-Smith:
Hairy Monsters & Nerdy Freaks

Neil Robinson:
Is There Anybody There? and *Short & Curly*

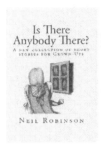 

Copies of this book, as well as the Kindle version, can be purchased on Amazon by searching 'Carlisle Writers'.